Tree of
WONDERS

Steve –
As you know, Florida
is an amazing place.

By GERALD L. GUY

GUY

www.storiesbyguy.com
Palm Coast, FL

Copyright

Tree of Wonders
Copyright © 2018 by Gerald L. Guy

This is a work of fiction. All the characters, names, locations, incidents, organizations and dialogue in this novel are either the products of the author's imagination or are used fictitiously. The views expressed in this work are solely those of the author.

ISBN-13: 978-1723558856
ISBN-10: 1723558850

Printed in the United States of America
AUTHOR: Gerald L. Guy
EDITOR: Fran McKiethan
COVER ART: Bigstock
PUBLISHER: www.storiesbyguy.com

Acclaim for Gerald L. Guy

Run Like the Wind

"I love Gus McIntyre! Gus, a 14-year-old boy traveling with his father to gold rush territory after they lost everything at home, is ambushed. His father is murdered. All their belongings are stolen. Gus is left for dead. Alone in the Wild West, Gus must depend on his personal strength and skills to survive in a lawless land. "Run Like the Wind" pulls you into this western coming of age story while entertaining and scaring you at the same time. This needs to be on TV."

Carol Ann Kauffman, Niles OH

Run to Danger

"I like this kid, Gus McIntyre! I love the way Gerald L. Guy draws you into a story and you can't leave until it's done. Gus stumbles upon a gang of rustlers that threaten the livelihood of the ranch he owes his life to. He sets out to return the cattle to the Circle H Ranch but needs the help of an old Apache Chief who befriends him. Times were tough. Gus has a maturity about him that even the old chief noticed and admired. They begin the journey together. A lot of twists and turns will keep you glued to the pages. A great read for teens and adults alike. I'm reading the third installment in this series and enjoying it every bit as much as the first two books! Thank you, Mr. Guy, for sharing your excellent story with us!

Juliette Douglas, Benton KY

Chasing Gold

"I thoroughly enjoyed "Chasing Gold." It was even more of a page-turner then your previous works, your best offering yet. Some of the twists and turns you put in there reminded me of another one of my favorite authors, Robert Ludlum. I have also read all his works.

I anxiously await the continuing adventures of young Gus as well as the third book in the "Wolf Pact" trilogy. I'll be checking your web site frequently so I can get signed up for pre-ordering as soon as possible.

Charlie Major, Palm Coast FL

Chasing the Past

"I love the Gus McIntyre series. Each book is filled with adventure, interesting characters and it won't let you put it down until the last page.

Author Gerald L. Guy weaves a colorful tapestry of fiction mingled with facts of when Gus' relatives travel to the new America and settling these fresh new lands. The whole series of Gus McIntyre is one you don't want to miss, I highly recommend! Good for Teens through adults!

Thank you, Mr. Guy, for sharing your wonderful storytelling with us!"

Juliette Douglas, Benton KY

SARA: A Hero's Story

My husband read and re-read this book. It brought back memories of his service aboard the Saratoga. He never talked much about his WWII experiences until "Sara" but then as he read, he explained so much. The book is like an old friend with whom he can relive experiences they shared.

Ami Lane, Palm Coast FL

Wolf Pact: The New Order

"Gerald L. Guy had the reputation of a hard-hitting newsman, not a guy who figures out how the appendix can explain his creatures' ability to transform from human to wolf. But he does so with a panache for fun with his novel, "Wolf Pact: The New Order."

Dean Poling, The Valdosta Daily Times

Altered Lives

Kept me guessing. Threads of story were well written and very entertaining.

Susan Popadak, Vero Beach, FL

Secrets of the Heart

I loved this story. You had me reaching for the Kleenex at the end.

Barbara Maddox, Buffalo NY

Novels by Gerald L. Guy

Gerald L. Guy is an independent author. His novels are available in multiple formats at online bookstores and his personal website. They include:

The McIntyre Adventures
Run Like the Wind
Run to Danger
PAYBACK: Eye for an Eye (Books 1&2)
Chasing Gold
Chasing the Past

Coastal Capers
Act of Kindness
Act of Mercy
Act of Recall

Wolf Pact saga
Wolf Pact: The New Order
Wolf Pact: Escape from Captivity
Wolf Pact: Dream Catchers

Other titles
Sara: A Hero's Story
Tree of Wonders
Secrets of the Heart
Altered Lives

www.storiesbyguy.com

TABLE OF CONTENTS

THE GERALD L. GUY COLLECTION

ACKNOWLEGEMENTS

Considerable research went into the writing of "Tree of Wonders." I could not have completed it without the extensive research of others, especially Peter Wohlleben, author of "The Hidden Life of Trees." His discoveries and insights into Mother Nature gave real legs to "Tree of Wonders."

I found a wealth of information in the works of William Ryan, historian and Flagler County resident. His "The Search for Old King's Road: The First Route into Florida" and "Bulow Gold" were tremendously informative. He has written several books on Flagler County history, a result of copious hours of research and discovery. I can't thank him enough.

His other novels include "I Am Gray Eyes: A Story of Old Florida," "Search for the Lost Plantations of Flagler County," and "Osceola: His Capture and Seminole Legends." If you want to learn more about the history of Flagler County and this region of Florida, his books are mandatory reading and available in paperback and electronic formats.

I culled considerable information from Les Standiford's "Last Train to Paradise." It gave me insight into the life and motivations of Henry Morrison Flagler, the man for which Flagler County is named. There isn't a great deal about him in "Tree of Wonder," but he was an amazing visionary who doesn't get enough credit for the civilized development of the Sunshine State at the close of the nineteenth century. He was the first to lay rail from Jacksonville to Miami and had the audacity to announce he would continue his rail service to Key West. It was called "Flagler's Folly," until he completed the task in 1912.

I also unearthed a treasure trove of historic data from "Tales of Old Florida," an anthology of historical accounts collected and edited by Frank Oppel and Tony Meisel.

Of course, online information is voluminous. But you'll find even more at the Flagler County Library and the many historical sites located throughout Flagler County. Stop by the libraries in Palm Coast or Flagler Beach once in a while. They have endless resources that are underused. Ditto for the Florida Agricultural Museum, Flagler Beach

Museum and the Holden House Museum in Bunnell, where people are dying to assist and educate.

You'll find footnotes that give credit to many sources of information that provided fodder for my stroll through Flagler's past. I hope you find them more informative than annoying.

The fact so much of Florida's rich history has been destroyed left me with a sour taste. The early plantation builders thought nothing of destroying Native American burial grounds. Modern developers were sometimes even less respectful as concrete highways and condominiums destroyed more historical evidence.

As a result, we know very little about the people who inhabited this beautiful peninsula centuries ago. If only those ancient Live Oak trees could speak to us and tell us about the people and activities that took place on this land before the white man arrived and plundered much of its natural wonders.

So, if you happen to find a seashell, an ancient arrowhead or the remnants of a rock foundation that seems out of place, notify the local historical society. It very well could be a link to a piece of Flagler County's great unknown.

www.storiesbyguy.com

DEDICATION

To the scores of volunteers and workers who toil each day to keep the parks and walking trails of Flagler County in beautiful condition. They make Flagler County superior to any place I have lived.

₁TREES

By Joyce Kilmer

I think that I shall never see
A poem lovely as a tree.

A tree whose hungry mouth is prest
Against the earth's sweet flowing breast.

A tree that looks at God all day
And lifts her leafy arms to pray.

A tree that may in Summer wear
A nest of robins in her hair.

Upon whose bosom snow has lain;
Who intimately lives with rain.

Poems are made by fools like me,
But only God can make a tree.
* * *

PREFACE

I first remember reciting Joyce Kilmer's "Trees" sometime during grade school. I think it was in Mrs. Landis' fifth-grade classroom. I don't know why it was my choice, other than it was short, had a rhythmic flow and represented my love of one of Mother Nature's most precious guardians. In those days, there was nothing I liked better than climbing to the top of a regal oak or elm, so I could watch the world from afar.

I was lucky to be raised in rural Ohio, a country boy. The Guy homestead stretched over 12 acres, most of which was populated by maple, poplar, beach, oak and elm trees. I also had access to the countryside that surrounded my family home, acres and acres of farm land and forests that begged exploration. Before I reached adolescence, I knew every square inch of that land, including in which trees bees liked to store their honey, which branches regularly supported bird nests and where I could see the farthest from the strongest branches. I spent many hours defending my tree fortifications from imaginary enemies and my older brother and his friends. It was a wonderful place to grow up.

Now, as an adult, I understand the importance of trees to our world and view them more fondly than ever. Of course, my travels have introduced me to scores of different species – the Catalpa or cigar tree, the Osage Orange used by Native Americans to make bows and arrows, the poisonous Buckeye, countless fruit trees, glorious palms and rambling banyans. I could go on and on because there are more than one thousand species of trees in North America. Next to the mighty Redwoods and Sequoias of California, I don't know if there is any tree more intriguing than the majestic Live Oaks that populate the Southeastern United States. Their far-reaching branches and enduring presence have captivated my imagination and given birth to "Tree of Wonders."

Live Oaks are known to live for centuries and are named such because they maintain their leaves all year, even in the winter when other oaks shed their greenery. The Angel Oak, near Johns Island, SC, is one of the nation's oldest. It has stood its ground for more than 1,500 years, scientists estimate. It stands at a height of more than 65 feet and spreads its branches in a canopy that measure more than 160 feet in diameter. History gives us glimpses of what this land was like 500 years ago. I can't imagine what it was like in 518 A.D. when the Angel Oak first began to grow.

I couldn't guess the age of some of the Live Oaks I have spotted along the scenic trails of Flagler County, Washington Oaks State Park and Princess Place. I was walking at Waterfront Park in Palm Coast one day when a line of stately Live Oak trees took my breath away. By their size, I could tell they were hundreds of years old, and a single thought crossed my mind: "Imagine what a five-hundred-year-old tree could tell a person if only it could talk." As I sat at my computer keyboard the next day, "Tree of Wonders" came to life.

When I discovered "The Hidden Life of Trees," written by [2]Peter Wohlleben, one might say my novel really found roots. The German author and forester shares a deep love of forests and explains the amazing processes of life, death, and regeneration he has observed in the woodlands of his native land. He also explains the amazing scientific wonders of tree life, an aspect few humans have considered. For instance, much like human families, Wohlleben explains, tree parents live together with their children, communicate with them and support them as they grow. They share nutrients with those who are sick or struggling and create an ecosystem that mitigates the impact of extreme heat or cold for the whole group. Because of these interactions, trees in a family or community are protected and can live to be very old, according to Wohlleben. In contrast, solitary trees, like street kids, have a tough time of it and, in most cases, die much earlier than those in a group.

Long ago, man recognized the leaves of most trees enriched the soil and improved crop growth. Scientists maintain the roots of trees exchange nutrients that sustain the soil and the plant life around them.

Some roots systems, such as the wild fig tree of South Africa, stretch downward for 400 feet or more. Trees can lift as much as 100 gallons of water per day out of the ground and discharge it into the atmosphere, making them fantastic partners in reducing storm water runoff and reducing air and water pollution,

Most of mankind admires the tree for the simple shade it provides. Few realize its role in the sustaining life because it cannot communicate with us. Or maybe we just do not understand the language of trees. I think Mother Nature is overflowing with amazing things we simply are not smart enough to comprehend. She waits patiently for humans to further evolve so her soft whisper can be understood.

So, I hypothesize that Wohleben is correct. Trees not only rule the forests, they communicate. They warn man of severe and natural weather changes; provide many species with food, shelter and medicine; protect our environment from a variety of threats; and, if we listen closely enough, speak with the wisdom and knowledge of the ages. If you don't believe me, just ask Willie Brown. You'll meet him in the very first Chapter.

CHAPTER 1

I have been coming to the coastal wetlands of Flagler County for longer than I can remember. My friends used to say I was the biggest fool this side of St. Augustine back when I was young. But I thought I was the lucky one. Before the sun was too high in the sky, I'd wrap a baloney sandwich in waxed paper, grab an orange from a tree outside our door and head east as fast as my feet would carry me. My destination was the East Coast Canal, now part of Florida's Intracoastal Waterway.

I was just nine or ten years old when I first discovered the animal trail that led to the canal. It allowed me to pass through the marshlands unscathed and arrive at the waterway in no time. Long before these bones got old and tired, I could run faster than most boys my age. I could make it to my favorite spot along the canal in less than thirty minutes if I just walked at a brisk pace. Most times, though, I ran because I could hear the waterway calling me.

There were few houses or condominiums lining that liquid thoroughfare in the 1960s when I first began visiting. It was just farmland and swamp. The canal was a busy place, though. It was used mainly for shipping goods from Jacksonville to Daytona and farther south. Why a body had no idea what he might see passing up and down the waterway in those days. Now, the traffic is dominated by big cabin cruisers, fishing boats and jet-skis.

I went there because it was quiet and cool. Eighty- and ninety-degree days are common in Florida and especially at my family's home. Inland, the heat was oppressive; it felt like it hit triple digits every day. But on the banks of the East Coast Canal, the temperature felt ten to fifteen degrees cooler because a relentless breeze made you smile the minute you emerged from the wild underbrush that lined both sides of that azure highway.

Sometimes when the fish were running, I'd catch me a drum or a crappie and be happier than mama on Christmas morning. You see, drum don't want to be caught, and they put up a bit of a fight. Crappie too, but they never were too big. When a two- or three-pound drum hit, I imagined I was fighting Moby Dick.

1

Have you read or even know of "Moby Dick?" It was mandatory reading when I was a lad. It's a literary classic, written by [4]Herman Melville in the nineteenth century. He was a long-winded old cuss who penned a thrilling tale about the voyages of the *Pequod*, a whaling ship steered by an angry old salt, named Captain Ahab. He was on a relentlessly pursuit of a great Sperm Whale he called Moby Dick. Experts back then liked to debate which of the characters was most evil, the elusive whale or Ol' Captain Ahab. I voted for Ahab, because I've never seen a fish yet that liked to be poked and prodded by man.

Along my favorite fishing spot at the East Coast Canal was a big, old Live Oak Tree, the kind that added to the Florida mystique in the days following WWII when Americans were first discovering the wonders of the Sunshine State and flocking here like cotton-pickers to lemonade. There I go putting my age on display again. Most Floridians don't know a thing about cotton or lemonade. Most of you have never seen cotton in the field nor tasted fresh-squeezed lemonade. When I was a boy and the sun was scorching hot, there was nothing better than lemonade freshly picked from the trees on our land. My daddy was a tradesman but we always had a garden and lots of fruit trees on the Flagler property we rented.

I'm getting sidetracked here. So, back to my canal.

Sometime after my thirteenth birthday, that big, old Live Oak and I became friends. It stretched and towered over the area I liked to visit. She provided more than shade after my long runs; she welcomed me to my destination. When it was cold and blustery in the winter, she offered up her branches and trunk as shelter. And when I was in a bad mood, why I imagine that tree knows more about me than my own family.

You might be laughing and thinking this old coot has lost his mind. Believe me. I'm as clear-headed as a preacher on Sunday morning. And I've never had a friend more loyal or trustworthy than that majestic Live Oak. Whenever it commenced to thunder and rain, sometimes at the drop of a hat, I'd run under that oak for protection and it never failed me. If I had a hankering to look all the way down the canal to Daytona Beach, she'd let me climb all the way up into her crown and present me with a view that was downright breathtaking. I'd climb up there right now if I wasn't so darn old. And just don't ask,

2

because it's none of your business exactly how old I am. Frankly, my age sometimes distresses me.

I remember clearly the summer day me and that tree became intimate friends. It was a warm one, the kind that made your shirt stick to your back the minute you stepped outside. My father, who served in the U.S. Navy during the big war, called those kind of days "equatorial." It is a word he fashioned to commemorate when that big ship of his crossed the equator and the heat was so intense it just about melted the paint right off the flight deck.

You see, almost all our fathers fought in World War II. They were proud of the job they did against Hitler and those brutal and demented warriors of the Rising Sun. My daddy signed up the day after Japan bombed Pearl Harbor and served most of his time chasing the enemy across the Pacific Ocean. He never talked much about his service, but when he saw me in those khaki military slacks, the smile on his face looked as if it was big enough to stretch all the way to Iwo Jima, where his ship took one heck of a beating. So, I wore them constantly — clean or dirty, tattered or torn.

I loved it when he used to tell me about the times he and his buddies scrambled eggs right on the wing of one of those bombers while they waited in line to take off and torment the Japanese. My father worked below deck, but he witnessed hundreds of take-offs, landings and crashes on the deck of that old carrier.

My father served his entire enlistment aboard the *U.S.S Saratoga CV-3*, one of only three aircraft carriers in the U.S. fleet prior to the bombing of Pearl Harbor in 1941. It was en route to Hawaii at the time of the attack and fortunately was not caught in the fiery onslaught that killed so many of our innocent young men. It left a lasting impression on my father and an imprint on his son. To this day, those veterans remain this country's greatest heroes in my estimation. I know it's a debatable statement, depending upon whether you had a loved one serve in the military or not.

I did my stint in the U.S. Air Force but didn't see any real action. I was a paper-pusher, much as I was for most of my civilian career. I liked to tell stories, and it's time I get back on track with this one. Now, where was I?

Believe it or not, I came to the canal that day packing a paperback copy of "Moby Dick." It was summer, but I knew it was mandatory reading for my upcoming eighth-grade English class in the fall. I wanted to get a jump on it because everyone said it was difficult reading. They were right, too. I wasn't liking it much. That book was too large to fit into my hip pocket. So, I had to slip it into the side pocket on the military pants all the guys wore back then because they were cool.

I liked them because those side pockets were large enough to carry a day's worth of sandwiches, an orange, some bubble gum and a handkerchief my mother insisted I carry without fail. The other side was suitable for Melville's "Moby Dick," my pocket knife and granddad's compass.

At any rate, I didn't have much luck fishing that day. So, I climbed up into the branches of my favorite Live Oak and turned to page 230 of Melville's manuscript. The most impressive thing about my Live Oak was its size. I figured it must have been five hundred years old, because I could sit comfortably on one of its massive branches, lean my back against its trunk and be more comfortable than if I was sitting on the front porch in my daddy's rocking chair. Shucks, as far as I was concerned, the view was a whole lot better, too.

Well, I commenced to reading as Ahab continued his maniacal pursuit of Moby Dick. The thing about Melville, you see, it takes him a couple pages to say what I could explain in one sentence. It wasn't the fastest-moving commentary; in fact, it was darn boring. But I pressed on. I had to if I wanted to get a passing grade in English when school started.

Before you know it, Herman put me right to sleep. I didn't wake up until a cranky old owl screeched to tell me I was a bit out of place in the Flagler forest after dark. It scared the bejesus out of me because all I saw when my eyes opened was that owl's two big orbs staring at me like I was [5] Miss Havisham's wedding cake. My backside and feet were still firmly planted on the hefty branch I had stretched out on, half the moon was shining and there must have been a million stars looking down at me. It was a glorious view until I looked downward. Everything on the forest floor below me was as dark as Satan's heart and double-dog scary.

I knew the forest wasn't anywhere for me to be after dark. "Damnation!" I proclaimed. "I'm in big trouble now! Pa's going to skin me good!"

When the owl heard my voice, it cocked its head and screeched a second time. It sent chill bumps up both arms and down my spine. So, I reached into my cargo pocket for my pocket knife. I unfolded it and stabbed it into the limb where I was perched. I wanted it close just in case the owl decided to attack. The minute my blade penetrated the tree's bark, I swear that mighty oak groaned at me.

I looked down below and couldn't see anything or anyone who could have made such a sound. I had heard alligators growl and wolves snarl, but I had never heard anything as pitiful as the sound I heard when I stuck my blade into the limb that was going to provide me safe harbor for the night.

That's when my chill bumps started giving me a case of the trembles. So, I called out: "Is somebody out there? Show yourself!"

Lo and behold, the branch on which I sat began to sway ever so gently. Then, a soft and willowy voice replied. "How would you like it if I stuck one of my sharp branches in one of your appendages?"

"What?" I said, astonished.

"After all the time we've spent together, why would you stick a knife into one of my most trustworthy branches? Hasn't it supported your weight dozens of times and kept you very comfortable this entire afternoon?"

"Okay! This isn't funny anymore. Who are you and why are you trying to play a trick on me?" I asked. "I'm just a kid!"

"Take the knife out, and I'll tell you anything you want to know," the voice said.

"Right!"

Nonetheless, I leaned forward and removed the knife from the limb but kept it gripped tightly in my hand. Simultaneously the voice signed passionately and said, "Thank you."

I was so dumbstruck my mouth dropped open and I swear an army of mosquitoes must have marched down my throat because I started to cough and heave like a coal-miner on his death bed. When my convulsions subsided, tears were running down my cheeks and the owl still was staring at me. I got the feeling he was hoping I would keel over dead so he could have a midnight snack.

I pointed the blade at it and bravely said, "If you want a piece of me, it ain't going to come easy Mr. Owl. This knife is going to take a piece out of you if you get any closer. Now go find something a little smaller to chew on."

"He means you no harm, Willie," the voice said. "He's just not used to sharing his nighttime watch with a human. He stops by every night. You are the thing out of place here, boy," the voice said.

Without taking my eyes off the owl, I answered the voice. "Well, tree, if you really are talking to me, I'd appreciate it you send that owl packing. He's making me nervous. It's bad enough I fell asleep up here and won't be able to make it home in the dark. I don't need Mr. Owl staring at me all night."

"You're not alone, Willie," the voice said. "I'm here, just as I have been for hundreds of years. I won't let anything happen to you."

Before I could blink, a branch dropped down from above and pushed the owl from its perch. It flew away into the darkness, screeching again as if it had been maimed rather than encouraged to go elsewhere.

I couldn't believe my eyes. Without thinking, I said, "Thank you!" Then, I folded the pocket knife and placed it back in the cargo pocket of my pants before realizing how stupid I must have sounded. I had just thanked a tree.

"You are quite welcome, Willie," the voice replied. "Maybe if you had told me the owl scared you, I could have shooed it away without you stabbing me."

"Sorry!" I said. Of course, I didn't know what else to say. I'd never talked to a tree before.

"Just ask from now on. It's not like we're strangers. How long have you been coming here and enjoying the wonders of my limbs?"

I rubbed my eyes with my fists and shook my head to clear out whatever cobwebs remained from my sound slumber. I pinched myself. Sure enough; I was awake, and this wasn't a dream. I didn't answer right away, though. Answering would mean I was having a conversation with a tree, and I wasn't ready to admit that just yet.

"Willie, you have nothing to fear. You've been talking freely to me for a very long time. Isn't that one of the reasons why you come here? You like to unburden your soul of your youthful problems.

"Do you remember when that bully blackened your eye a few years back? I listened to your sorrows. And I sympathized with your laments when that baseball player surpassed Babe Ruth's home run record. I didn't say anything because you just needed to vent.

"Frankly, I've listened quietly for centuries. Now, when I've decided to have a conversation, you suddenly are silent. Why?"

Now, this was startling. Nobody could possibly have known the things I had said on my trips to the East Coast Canal. At least, I figured I was alone and nobody was listening. Holy cow! The tree not only knew my name, it new stuff. Personal stuff.

I didn't know whether to run or stay and engage the tree in a conversation. Her voice was so soft and comforting, it reminded me of how my mother sounded when she came to wake me up each morning to begin my chores. I decided to stay because I needed an explanation, and there was no way I was going to tramp through the swampy terrain between the East Coast Canal and my home in the dark.

"Okay, first tell me how this can be happening? Trees don't talk," I said in my most demanding voice.

"There are many things about Nature you do not know, young Willie Brown," the voice replied. "Because of my prominence in the forest and my long standing on this land, I am granted privileges other species are not. I don't overuse them but on occasion I get lonely, too. I just thought we were friends and, being you were most likely staying the night, we'd exchange a few friendly thoughts."

"Friends?"

"We are friends by nature of your repeated visits. My branches have supported you time and time again. Even this night, when you were most afraid, I protected you. Isn't that what friends do?"

"Oh, yeah. But you're a tree and I'm a boy."

"Well, I was young once, albeit many winters ago. I know what fear is like. You know, they almost chopped me down once when they were building this canal. That was pretty scary."

"Oh, wow! I'm sure glad they didn't. This place wouldn't be the same without you. I love it here," I replied. "And you're one of the reasons I keep coming back. You are big and beautiful, and you never disappoint me. I just can't believe we're having a conversation. Can you please explain that to me?"

"First you must understand, all things in nature are conversant. Every species has its own way of communicating. I know you have heard the wolves howl and even the owl screech; it's all a form of communication. At night, the crickets and frogs go on forever. Humans just can't understand any of what they are saying."

"Do you understand them?"

"Of course, I understand all of them. I'm the oldest living thing in this forest. I've been listening to them for centuries."

"Do you communicate with them, too?" I asked.

"Sometimes, but not often. I am a great listener, as you might confirm up until tonight, I have heard many tales and know many things," the tree replied.

"How are you able to communicate with me," I asked.

"As you can see, I have no mouth. But my spirit is strong, and it communes with your spirit, which I can sense the minute you contact any part of me. You are the first human I have shared thoughts with in more than two hundred and fifty years."

"Really? Do you have a name? What should I call you? Tree just sounds too unfriendly."

"My name is Sani. It was given to me by a human many years ago. He was native to this land and considered me holy. He prayed at my base regularly. His name was *Chiqua*, and he was the spiritual leader of the Timucuan tribe that settled in this area long before white people arrived."

"I've never heard of that tribe. Can you tell me more about them?" I asked.

"I will be glad to tell you all I know of the Timucuan, if you will tell me if your Captain Ahab slays this mighty whale he is chasing."

"Ah, you've been listening while I've been reading. What do you think so far?"

"I'm rooting for the whale, Willie. He is one of Nature's children and will have to outsmart this wily man of the sea. Perhaps Moby Dick can call on King Neptune to come to his aid."

"Different story and different part of the world, Sani. I don't think Neptune is going to come to the rescue of Moby Dick. But I'll come back and read you more, if you would like. It's kind of nice knowing someone is listening."

"And I will tell you of the Timucuan Indians who were the first humans to inhabit this land."

I spent the next few hours quizzing Sani about some of the things I had confessed to her during my visits to the canal, and she responded with all the correct answers. She even asked me about Clark Kent and Bruce Wayne, characters in the comic books I sometimes brought along to read while waiting for the fish to bite. And that was how we began to swap stories. I realized Sani knew many things, but her knowledge came from tiny spectrums of life that happened to wander near or under her branches.

She had never heard of heroes the likes of Batman and Superman, and found their stories intriguing because they spent all of their time "helping other humans."

While there were many things she had learned from the past, she knew very little about the trappings of the modern world we shared. As much as I loved hearing about the great things she had seen and heard while growing old along the Flagler County waterway, she was enchanted by the tales of men like Captain Ahab, King Arthur and even Clark Kent. Before we both fell asleep in the wee hours, our friendship was sealed by the knowledge we could share with each other.

Sani woke me at dawn and sent me on my way, but not without urging me to return and read more of "Moby Dick". I agreed but knew I would be away for a while. I was going to be grounded for the worry I had caused my parents.

Both of my parents were angry when I returned home. Momma made me promise not to do such a thing again and daddy took me to the shed and gave me a sample of what would happen if I did. It was humbling, and I was grounded for a week. But neither rain, sleet nor my daddy's belt could keep me from returning to the East Coast Canal whenever time allowed. Sani and me became more than just friends; we were buddies. You won't believe some of the tales that mighty oak shared with me. If you are interested, read on. I promise not to deviate from the truth, according to Sani.

CHAPTER 2

When I finally was allowed to leave my property for anything other than family outings, my reprimand fulfilled, I was eager to get back to the [1]East Coast Canal and talk with my new friend. Keep in mind, I withstood some very intense interrogation from my parents on what I was doing in the forest all night. I told them about my fears and the owl and the eerie noises that come alive in the wilderness after dark. However, I refused to mention a word about Sani. I was afraid I would be grounded for another week for telling such a horrific tale.

Nonetheless, I got a week to hash over my initial conversation with my Tree of Wonders. A million questions were percolating inside me when I arrived at the canal on a warm Saturday morning. I greeted Sani with a smile and climbed up into her welcome arms shortly after arriving. We talked briefly about my punishment and then I changed the subject to the natives who first settled in Flagler County. I wanted to know more about the [6]Timucua Indians Sani mentioned a week ago.

"Where exactly did those native people live?" I asked.

Sani didn't hesitate. She began to reveal some of Flagler County's rich history, stories I had never before heard. Keep in mind, these were all things she learned while standing in one place for centuries.

"They started with a small encampment not far from here, along what I used to call Timucua Creek because that is what attracted the natives to this location. They considered it their property and were very protective of it. It was a big part of their daily lives, providing both food and water for generations.

"Later, your predecessors named it Long Creek. Back then, the creek was as wide as I am tall and its waters ran swiftly. It nourished the entire region before winding its way south. The fish in that creek were so plentiful, there were times the Timucua children could cross the stream walking on the backs of the drum and bream that called those waters home.

"It was the fish that summoned the Timucua to this region. They were avid hunters of land animals, but it was the fish that sustained them. It was said the tribe's spirit-talkers would stand on the shores of the Atlantic and sing to the marine life until they swam into the shallow water where fierce warriors clubbed or speared them before

11

dragging them to shore for others to clean and prepare for consumption.

"The Timucua were a very advanced and civilized people. They welcomed everyone into their camps. While most families lived in their own shelters, the entire tribe gathered at the center of their encampments where food was prepared and eaten daily. As you can imagine, feeding dozens of people three times a day, required constant hunting and preparation.

"*Chiqua* told me his great-grandfather was one of the tribe's most famous spirit-talkers and a legendary fisherman. His name was *Ahanu*. Long before *Chiqua* was born, the people had endured a scorching spring and summer. I had horrible memories of it because it was a stain on my roots. Most of the creeks and smaller streams around here dried up. I had to drive my roots deep below the creek's bed to sustain myself. I was all I could do just to keep my leaves green.

"The Timucua's stores were bare, and the people were starving when *Ahanu* volunteered to cross the hammocks and summon food from the sea. *Ahanu* pounded on his chest and promised not to return without the largest fish in the sea. When he left the camp for his journey east, many of the warriors laughed at his brash promise.

"For three days and three nights, *Ahanu* sang to the God of the Deep, begging him to send a great fish to save the Timucua people from starvation. *Ahanu* was weak and near exhaustion when, on the morning of the fourth day of his quest, the sun peaked over the shining blue waters and he saw a dark mass forming far out to sea. *Ahanu* waded into the water so only his head floated above the waves as the dark mass approached.

"As the darkness got closer, the spirit-talker thought it was a massive wave, darker than any he had seen before. *Ahanu* tried to flee, but it was too late. He cried out in fear when he saw a spray of water shoot straight up from the crest of the wave and a whale open its gigantic mouth. As the wave crashed upon him, he was swallowed by the creature. Gobbled up, he prayed his gods would not abandon him. And they did not

"The wave deposited the whale on the shoreline where it became beached when the waves receded. The whale had no way of returning to its watery domain. With one final gasp, the mighty king of the ocean exhaled from its blowhole and spit out the spirit-talker. *Ahanu,* too, was gasping for air but took time to thank his gods for saving his life and heeding his plea.

"*Ahanu* marveled at the size of the creature. It was larger than the biggest lodge at his camp. He stood atop its tail and crawled across its back. When he reached the highest point, he pulled a conch shell from the travel bag strapped to his torso and blew into it as hard as he could. It was a signal that a tribesman was in trouble and needed help.

"Over and over he blew into the conch until the entire village emptied and came to the seashore. When they saw him standing atop the mighty whale, his people were amazed, and *Chiqua's* great-grandfather never again was a target of laughter. His tale of being swallowed by the great whale was told and retold for many generations."

"What did they do with such a great catch?" I asked.

"*Chiqua* said it took the tribe many days to harvest the great beast. They built dozens of fires on the beach to cook its savory meat. After they ate their fill, the women carried huge chunks of it back to their camp where it was smoked and preserved for the coming winter. The males heated the blubber in clay pots for oil the tribe used for cooking and trading during winter. Whale oil also was used in the tanning of the deerskins they all wore.

"The whale's bones became tools the tribe used to farm the land and defend themselves against enemies. The Timucua believed the whale was a sacred gift from the Great Spirit. Everyone carried with them a piece of bone they carved and polished in commemoration of day the tribe's starvation came to an end, thanks to *Ahanu. Chiqua* had a small piece of bone that once belonged to his legendary grandfather. It was more than one hundred years old, and he wore it proudly around his neck for all to see. He cherished it more than life itself."

I was amazed by the story and begged Sani not to stop. I told her it reminded me of a biblical tale my mother told me when I was just a child. As I recall God wanted Jonah to be a prophet, but he refused and went to sea instead. When a storm struck, he was saved from drowning when he was swallowed by a whale. He survived in the belly of the whale for three days and three nights before the whale spit him out onto a desolate beach. Thankful to be alive, [7]Jonah accepted God's direction and fulfilled his mission of prophecy, my mother said.

"I have heard that story before, Willie," Sani said. "I've always thought it was amazing how human legends seem to intertwine and spread wide to people of different nationalities."

"Me too," I replied. "It makes you wonder if there isn't some truth to the legends, and there is a Great Spirit or God out there directing all that happens to mankind. It seems people of all religious believe in some kind of higher power."

"I know only of the spirit that unites all living things. I feel it from my roots to my leaves. It is very powerful, and it is one of the reasons I am able to communicate with so many species."

I didn't want to get into a philosophical conversation about religion. I wanted to hear more about the Native Americans who inhabited the lands long before the white man invaded. So, I urged Sani to tell me more of the Timucua tribe and listened intently.

"Unlike you, the Timucua covered their bodies only when the temperature cooled in the fall and winter. The men and women wore tiny cloths, made of leather or woven from plants, to protect their lower bodies, but most of their bodies were exposed to the sun. Clothing was not considered a necessity. The natives not only welcomed the scorching sun but they worshiped it. They believed the sun toughened their skin and made them resistant to insect bites and some of the infectious plant life. When winter came, they dressed in deerskins, and the tribe huddled as families in their lodges. Inside, fires blazed, and the skin of Florida's black bear kept them warm.

"While the Timucua were avid fisherman, they also were tactical hunters. They worshiped the black bear for it was their most fierce adversary. They needed its fur and fat to sustain their lives when the ocean winds grew cold and frigid. The hunters strung the bear's claws around their necks as a sign of bravery, and never departed on a bear hunt without great ceremony. They prayed to their gods to keep their hunters safe and for the hunt to be successful. Many times, they did it right here under my branches.

"Of course, they came to me for medicine, too. The Timucua boiled my leaves to heal wounds and ease swelling. They made tea with my bark to soothe aching teeth and stomach ailments. The tribal women ground my bark into a powder that stopped bleeding almost immediately. I didn't mind, because they never took more than what was needed. They paid me back twofold."

"How so?" I asked. "I know your wood is very strong. The Indians must have been in awe of your great size."

"Oh, I am large, but my roots run ten times farther than my branches will ever reach," Sani explained. "They were fed by the creek that once passed through this land. When the Timucua arrived, I already was the largest of my species. The Indians worshipped me because of my great size and medicinal value. It was they who made great spurts of growth possible. The Timucua buried fish along my root system, from which I found great nourishment. We lived in harmony for centuries. As my branches rose higher and higher and my trunk expanded, so did the Timucua. They believed I was a gift from their gods, and they fed me far more than I could consume. Many of the tribe's spiritual leaders erected altars at my base. Their chiefs held court in the shade of my great canopy."

I had to interrupt Sani's story to tell her about the Pilgrims who first came to this land on the Mayflower, a great sailing ship that took many weeks to cross from Europe to the New World.

"It is a wonderful story, one that reminds me of the tales I have heard of the Native Americans who greeted the [8]Pilgrims when they landed at Plymouth Rock," I said. "They had lived on their lands for centuries but did not welcome the Europeans as warmly as the Timucua did. They instantly became enemies until they learned to live together in peace. Eventually, the natives taught the Pilgrims how to live and prosper in their new home. At harvest time, a big feast was held to give thanks. We still celebrate it in November. It is called Thanksgiving.

"But I must apologize again for interrupting. I thought you would find my story interested. I still am intrigued by your stories about these native people because they lived right here. Please go on. I want to learn more.

"What happened to the Timucua?" I asked.

"I am getting there. Be patient, Willie Brown. We have all day.

"As generations came and went, the tribe migrated out of respect for the other creatures that inhabited the region. The Great Drought taught the dangers of overhunting the lands. So, as the numbers of the Timucua grew, they spread far and wide. Their native lands stretched far to the west and south. They rarely fought with neighboring tribes and embraced all travelers to their camps. It was their peace-loving nature that led to their demise. They perished like the unpicked fruit of the orange tree, their beauty bringing about their own demise."

"How could so many just disappear?" I asked.

"*Chiqua* was the last shaman of the First People to worship at my base," Sani told me. "At his birth, thousands of his people roamed these lands, as it had been for many generations. I was just beginning to feel the strength in my limbs when I first noticed the Timucua walking this forest.

"When the Spanish arrived on the shores of the Atlantic, they brought with them diseases the innocent Timucua could not withstand. You must understand, the people of this land suffered normal bumps and bruises. Food- and plant-related illness were common, but they never suffered from the respiratory problems introduced by the Spanish invaders. The Timucua had no natural resistance to the germs the visitors brought to their campfires. Until that time, the Timucua had never had so much as a cold.

"It was *Chiqua* who led the Spanish explorer Juan Ponce de Leon to me for shelter from a sudden rain storm. By that time, hundreds of his people had died from [9]influenza and small pox. It ran through their villages like the water of Timucua Creek.

"*Chiqua* tried to explain to the Spaniard that his followers carried a sickness that not even the healing properties of my leaves would cure. The conquistador was obstinate and uncaring. The Spanish leader was searching for his precious Fountain of Youth and he cared little that his men raped the land and the people in search of riches. Three months after the Spanish abandoned these shores, the Timucua were no more. *Chiqua* collapsed and died at my base. His body was drug off by a pack of wolves who consumed him and then died of the disease that his flesh transmitted.

"He was a good man, and I have spent many years silently grieving his death. Then, you arrived at this place I have called home for so long and ignited in me the lust for friendship once again. I am glad, and I hope you return often to my branches for conversation. There are many experiences we both can share."

"I am overjoyed you have chosen me to befriend, Sani," I replied. "I promise to come here as often as possible. I love this spot. It's my little paradise and you are its grandest inhabitant. Know one thing, though, my parents will grow angry if I fall asleep here again and do not return home before nightfall. They will kill me. So, don't let me fall asleep here again. I won't be able to come back if I do."

"Why would your parents murder you?" Sani asked.

"They wouldn't do that. They love me. I was using a figure of speech to exaggerate. I should have said punish instead of kill. Sorry!"

"Ah, you scared me. I know humans bury one another when they die. I feared you were in great danger."

"No! No! You are funny, Sani." I replied. "My parents would ground me for a month if I caused them worry again."

"Well, tell them Sani was watching out for you, and they should not worry."

"I don't think they will believe such a story; nobody will trust a word from my mouth if I tell them my newest friend is a giant Live Oak. It will have to be *our* secret."

"You are nothing like *Chiqua*," Sani replied. "He told everyone in his tribe of our conversations. I think that is why they came to worship me so. I miss my Timucua friends."

"Well, I'll be a better friend than *Chiqua*, Sani. I have had immunizations from most diseases. So, with luck, I'll travel back and forth as your friend for many years to come."

"And that makes me very happy," Sani replied, her big branches swaying on a windless afternoon.

CHAPTER 3

By the time I returned to the Sani's huge branches I was almost finished with "Moby Dick". I hoped Sani was in a mood to listen to the story as it concluded. So, I curled up on my favorite branch, leaned against her massive trunk and provided an update on the story. Melville had picked up the pace as the climax loomed. Sani didn't respond to me right off. So, I just opened Melville and started reading aloud.

It was a still day but I felt Sani coming to life as grisly old Ahab launched his third and final assault on the great white whale. The branch beneath me undulated when Ahab's words tumbled from my lips: "Towards thee I roll, thou all-destroying but unconquering whale; to the last I grapple with thee; from hell's heart I stab at thee; for hate's sake I spit my last breath at thee."

"The man surely was mad, Willie Brown," my old friend said as clearly as the sun shined from the Florida sky.

"I didn't know if you were listening or not," I said. "Yeah, old Ahab is nuttier than my grandma's fruit cake."

"Fruit cake?"

"Oh, sorry. You wouldn't know what that is. It is a delicacy made at Christmastime by my grandmother. It's made with flour, eggs, sugar and some spices. Grandma fills hers with dried fruit and nuts. Then she soaks it in rum until it has lots of flavor. Grandpa loves it. I don't care much for it, though."

"Ah, I know all about sugar, Willie. Before the canal was built, I was told this land once contained sugar cane fields for as far as the human eye could see. It was during the time the British claimed Florida as their property. They thought Florida's warm and humid weather would be perfect for cultivating the stalks they discovered in China and brought them to these lands.

"The British were a greedy bunch. Planters stood right beneath these branches and plotted how and where they would plant their crops. They thought if they could grow their own sugar cane here, it would be cheaper than importing it from halfway around the world. They all had visions of great wealth."

"Sani, how do you know all this?" I asked.

"Young man, just because I don't know how old I am, doesn't mean I know nothing about history. As long as I have stood next to this waterway, I've been listening to your people babble about one thing or another. Don't think you're the first human to climb up into my branches and read. I've not only observed history, I've absorbed it.

"The sap that runs through every limb and leaf I produce is very powerful. When you lean against my bark, that fluid is heated by your body and it creates the bond that allows us to communicate. I can read every thought that goes through your mind. So, when you're reading "Moby Dick" silently, the words are transferred to me. But please don't stop reading aloud. I do love to listen as you tell a story."

"Well, shut my mouth, Sani!" I declared. "You really are amazing. I promise to bring a book along on most of my visits. I like reading and, now that I know you always are listening, it will be much more enjoyable."

"Oh, Willie, you are a good friend. You are welcome in my branches any time," the tree whispered to my brain.

"Tell me more about this sugar crop, though. I've sort of taken sugar for granted. It's always there when I want it, and I've never thought about how it got to the kitchen table in my house. I certainly didn't know you could grow sugar cane in this part of Florida," I said.

"Well that was during the time when the Europeans were fighting over the possession of Florida. The Spanish, French and English all offered huge land grants to countrymen who were brave enough to come here and till the soil for the rich kings and queens who lived far from here. Sugar was highly sought after. Prior to its discovery in China, honey was the only sweetener available, and I'm sure you know how ornery bees can be. In those years, much of the land north and south of here contained field after field of sugar cane.

"A rich planter, named Maj. Charles Wilhelm Bulow, acquired an old Spanish land grant south of here and parlayed it into six thousand acres. He planted some cotton and rice on his fertile land, but most of it was dedicated to raising sugar cane. He brought three hundred slaves with him to build a sugar mill and tend his crops.

"Before I tell you about that sugar cane, though, I have to tell you about the Creek Indians. They followed the Timucua people into this countryside and they were nothing like the First People I got to know when I was centuries younger. By the time the Creeks got to Florida, they were a fractured and warring nation. They were castoffs and runaways from a variety of tribes – Creeks, Yuchis, Yamasses and a few others – which had resided in Tennessee, Alabama and western Florida. They became known as Seminoles, a name that meant 'wild people' or 'runaway.'

"They kept moving east until they found a territory where they could live the kind of life they chose. Once they got here, there was no resistance because the Timucua already had traveled to the Great Beyond. Unlike their friendly predecessors, the Seminoles were extremely territorial and fought hard to protect their lands from invaders, especially the white man. They quite often took whatever they wanted, but nobody stole from the Seminoles.

"They camped right here along this waterway for many years. Not far from here, they performed their ritual dances and applied their war paint over and over. They came to me to beg for strength and drink the tea, made from my leaves. They believed my leaves would make them strong in battle. I must admit, they triumphed most of the time and lost far fewer lives than their enemies. I like to think my tea had something to do with their success.

"Unlike the Timucua who congregated in large masses, the Seminoles preferred camps of four to six families. Their villages were small but not defenseless. They used drums and smoke signals to communicate with other villages throughout the region. If there was trouble, a signal went out and warriors from all the villages responded.

"Once, a large number of Choctaw Indians sneaked down the creek at night and tried to surprise the Seminoles. One of the Seminole braves had stolen a Choctaw maiden and refused to return her. The Choctaws thought they could take her back by force. While being outnumbers two-to-one, the Seminoles not only repelled the attack but they tracked and killed every native who took part. It was a bloodbath. This creek ran red for days, I was told. Most of the animals refused to drink from it.

"When the white man again began arriving on the shores of the Atlantic and driving their ships and boats down the St. John's River into this country, the Seminoles defended their property rights and refused to give a speck of land to any settlers. But it was a losing battle. The whites came in great numbers and soon outnumbered the Seminoles.

"The Seminoles were fearsome warriors. *Hana* was the spiritual leader of the tribe, and he visited me frequently. My thick branches were impressive and he stepped beneath them a bit wary the first time. I was the largest tree he had ever seen and he was unsure if my spirit was good or evil because my branches stretched in so many directions. He built a small fire at my base and began chanting and dancing. I had seen such activities before. So, I shook my leaves and made my branches sway to convince him I had great power. It worked and I was revered by the entire Seminole nation. From that time on, their leaders came to me when they prayed to their gods.

"They begged the spirits to drive the white man from their midst, but it was futile. They often gathered here. Warriors from many villages painted their bodies, drank my tea and struck out in raiding parties to attack the trespassing white men and their families."

"Weren't you afraid of them?" I asked.

"Of course not. I am bigger and stronger than most species. I have withstood droughts, floods, tornadoes, locusts, disease and greedy lumbermen. The Seminoles would have to work very hard to destroy me, but they never tried. Years later, the white man did, though."

"I'm guessing that's when they were building this canal," I replied.

"Yes, but that is a story for another day, Willie."

"I'm sorry. Tell me more about the Seminoles. I've read about the Seminole Wars in my Florida History class."

"Then you know the Seminoles were a brutal people. They took scalps, beheaded and disemboweled their enemies. They'd present the remains of their unfortunate victims to me. Often, they came here to thank me and their gods for the strength given them in battle. It was a horrible time for the whole region. I withdrew from the human interaction because the Seminoles so repulsed me.

"Their war against the white man took its toll on the tribe eventually. Even though they must have killed hundreds of men, women and children, their actions got the attention of the U.S. Army. When the soldiers showed up, the Indians' tiny raids against unsuspecting settlers turned into a war."

"Why didn't the white settlers ban together and run the Seminoles off?" I asked.

"They were farmers looking for fertile land and a peaceful life in the warm climates of Florida. The dream of growing crops twelve months of the year lured them here. Most carried rifles for protection, but they were no match for the Seminoles who were tactical and fearless warriors.

"I knew the Seminoles' time was drawing to a close the first time [10]Andrew Jackson stood beneath my limbs and addressed his troops about the need to avenge the atrocities of the Seminole Indians, I knew the human landscape of the countryside was about to change again."

"Are you saying Andrew Jackson came here to Florida?" I asked.

"He sure did. He was a great military leader and orator. His soldiers loved him. He was sent here to quell the uprising and relocate the Seminoles to lands far from here. He stood at my base and marveled at my size, just as you and many others have, Willie. And it was at this spot he exhorted his troops to shoot straight and drive the Seminoles from these lands. He made each of them swear to die trying.

"It wasn't long after Jackson stood under my branches that *Hana* returned with a band of one hundred or more Seminoles. He told his followers the cavalry had found sanctuary at the large sugar plantation along [11]Bulow Creek, just south of here. They were right. Some of the soldiers set up encampments on the large plantations where provisions were plentiful, and the infestations and vermin of Florida's harsh wilderness were at least bearable.

"I had overheard merchants and passersby say the Bulow Plantation was the largest in all of Florida. For two days, the Seminoles danced and painted their bodies in preparation for their attack on the plantation. The mightiest warriors painted their bodies white with black and red stripes. They were the most fearsome humans to ever walk beneath my branches and I felt sorry for the soldiers they sought to destroy.

"No soldiers were at the plantation, though. But it didn't matter. The Seminoles killed everyone who resided or worked there, women, children, slave and overseer. Then, they ransacked the place and burned most of it to the ground.

"That was the beginning of the end for the Seminoles. More troops were sent to quell the marauding 'wild ones.' Jackson returned and again addressed his troops beneath my branches. I remember his words exactly. He said, 'War is a blessing, compared to the degradation perpetrated by the Seminole Nation against innocent Americans. If they won't leave these lands willingly, we'll kill every last man of them.'

"And they almost did. Jackson became the marauder, attacking and killing natives throughout the region. Eventually, the Seminoles took to hiding in the swamps where the troops were afraid to follow.

"The Seminoles eventually made their homes in the Everglades where they could live in harmony with nature. They were determined not to leave Florida under any circumstances. By that time, the tribe had been joined by a large number of runaway slaves and black freedmen. They were worn down and pretty well beaten by the Blue Coats, as they called them.

"They stopped back here to pray to their gods and bid me farewell by stripping off most of my leaves. The youngest braves climbed through my limbs to secure the sacred leaves they would use to provide strength on their long journey. I didn't know if I would survive the sudden loss of energy they caused. Needless to say, I was glad to see them depart."

"I've walked through the remnants of the Bulow Plantation, just south of here," I confessed to Sani. "It's been preserved as an historic landmark in Flagler County. I knew the inhabitants had been killed in an Indian attack, but I did not know why. The Seminole Wars occurred more than a century ago, and the arrival of Ponce De Leone was early in the 1500s. That means you must be more than five hundred years old."

"Oh, I am much older than that, my friend. Have you forgotten about the First People, the Timucuans? They lived here long before the white explorers showed up on Florida's coast. I am most certainly twice that or older."

"That is amazing, Sani," I said. "It is hard for me to imagine being fifty years old. You may have existed for one thousand or more."

"Many have died over those years," Sani admitted. "Sometimes I wonder why I have been chosen to survive."

"Perhaps you are part of a bigger plan and meant to see this land move from violence to peace, to see people live side by side without killing each other," I suggested.

"Oh, this land has seen its share of violence. The massacre at Bulow Plantation was terrible, but there have been more heinous acts. What occurred much earlier where the St. John's River empties into Mosquito Bay was equally vicious but perpetrated by the Spanish against the French. As a result, the bay was renamed Matanzas Inlet, according to the people who have traveled this waterway.

"Before I tell you that tale, why don't you read more of "Moby Dick". We must find out if the great whale escapes the fanatical Captain Ahab? That story has stretched on long enough."

I wanted to know what happened, too. So, I just leaned my back against Sani's comfortable trunk and read the final Chapter aloud. By the time I got to the part where the whale destroys the *Pequod* and kills everyone but Ishmael, the narrator, I swear Sani's branches were swaying in celebration.

I looked around quizzically and asked, "Is a storm picking up, Sani, or are you just happy with the ending?"

"Oh, I am happy for Moby Dick," she replied. "But a storm is building on the horizon. You had best begin your journey home, Willie Brown, or you will be caught in what looks like a dandy of a storm."

I climbed down from my comfortable perch and couldn't help but notice the afternoon air was as calm as could be. It was hot, and the air was thicker than the black coffee my daddy drank each morning before heading off to work. Before leaving, I turned to Sani and said, "I want to thank you for a great afternoon, Sani."

"Oh, I enjoyed it, too, Willie. There is no reason to thank me."

"Are you sure it's going to rain?" I asked.

"I am very sure. I promise you'll be wet before you reach home, Now, move along quickly, Willie Brown, and bring another book when you return."

Before I could move, one of Sani's big branches swooped down and tapped me on my britches and nudged me on my way. It was so graceful, I marvel when I think of it to this day.

Oh, yeah! By the time I got to the top of the path the led to my family's home, the rain began to fall. I got wet, just like Sani predicted. I was convinced she really was a tree of wonders.

CHAPTER 4

It was several days later when I returned to Sani with another literary classic stuck into the cargo pocket of my military pants. This time it was "[12]The Adventures of Huckleberry Finn," one of my favorites. My friend had spent centuries next to a creek, and I thought she would like to learn of the misadventures of a resourceful young boy and a runaway slave cast afloat on the Mississippi River.

But Sani also had lit a fire in me to pursue local history. I went to the Public Library every chance I had to do some sleuthing into the background of the north-central region of Florida that we both loved. Lo and behold I came upon a gem I thought would surprise my statuesque friend. It seems the last naval battle of the American Revolution was waged near Cape Canaveral back in the eighteenth century.

I had no idea of the depth of my friend's knowledge, but I had never heard the story of this battle and couldn't wait to spring it on Sani the next day.

America was just shy of two centuries old when I was a boy, and I doubted Sani could have sensed the rumble of the cannons from that far away, but somebody might have been traveling down the creek and revealed to her details of the legendary battle at sea. Canaveral was about one hundred miles south of us and, no matter how high you climbed into her boughs, one could not see that huge port from Flagler County. Nonetheless, I was eager to tell Sani about my discovery from March 10, 1783.

If you know anything about American history, you know the fight for American freedom began in 1776 and ended in 1781 at the Battle of Yorktown. So, how could this naval confrontation mark the end of hostilities with Great Britain? I figured word of the British surrender traveled slowly through the Colonies and spread even more reluctantly across the Atlantic. Or maybe the Brits were as greedy as Sani had told me, and they just refused to give up their holdings in the New World.

History tells us the Continental Army of General George Washington suffered greatly during the war, and they fought on for five long years with very little food or pay. The fledgling nation just didn't have any money.

[13]Well, in 1783, two American ships – the *Alliance* and the *Duc de Lauzun* – left Cuba with seventy-two thousand Spanish silver dollars Washington intended to use to pay his bedraggled troops. The *Alliance* was one of the fiercest battleships of its day. The frigate was outfitted with thirty-six big cannons and had distinguished itself repeatedly during the War for Independence, mainly under the captaincy of fabled John Paul Jones. When it sailed along the coast of Florida, it was under the command of John Barry.

The *Duc De Lauzun* was basically a cargo ship that had been dispatched from Philadelphia to carry the silver, along with other commodities that were of equal value, to America. She was under the command of Captain John Green.

Somewhere along the Florida coast, the Americans spotted three British warships. Ordered to deliver the silver at all costs, the Spanish bullion was transferred to the *Alliance* and the *Duc* was stripped of most of its twenty cannons to lighten its load and allow it to flee north with commodities and her sister vessel. But the *Duc* was still too slow to escape. Barry gave the order to abandon the *Duc* and its crew to a certain death in lieu of assuring the delivery of the rich cargo to Philadelphia.

Instead of continuing its slow flight with the *Alliance*, Captain Green turned his smaller ship to defend against the fast-closing British Man of War, *Sybil*. Green's crew fired what cannon they had left, hoping to slow the enemy's pursuit and ensure the *Alliance's* escape. The bravery of Green's decision emboldened Barry and the crew of the *Alliance*, which refused to see their countrymen pummeled by the much larger vessel. The *Alliance* joined the fray and, with a broadside volley, crippled the *Sybil* and allowed the two American vessels to complete their mission successfully.

In reward for his valor in the face of certain death, Captain Green was given the helm of the *Empress* when it became the first American vessel to fly the flag of the United States of America on a trade journey to China, a vital mission to open trade between the two countries.

A month later, the *Duc De Lauzun* carried valuable French patriots, who had supported the American war effort, back to their homeland. Also aboard was Ambassador Ben Franklin, who would thank France for its assistance and report news of Cornwallis' surrender.

I couldn't wait to tell Sani of my discovery. As I climbed up into her branches, she addressed me immediately.

"My, I detect great joy emanating from your soul, Willie. What has brought you so much happiness on this beautiful day?" she asked.

"I have a surprise for you," I replied.

"I am centuries old and have seen many things," Sani replied. "There is not much that can surprise me."

"Maybe surprise is the wrong word," I said. "I am aware of your love of a good story. You have been enlightening me to the history of this region for weeks now. Today, I bring a story for you."

"Oh, I hope you have brought with you another novel. I so love it when you read to me."

"I've brought 'Huck Finn' with me, but that's not what has me so excited," I said. "I did some research and discovered a famous naval battle took place not far from here and I wanted to tell you about it."

"Do tell, Willie. Over the years I can recall only one such battle off this coast, and it led to a grisly outcome for the survivors. Of course, the rumble of faraway cannon easily can be felt on clear days. Such eruptions are not good for Nature. It upsets the flow of energy, stymies growth and sends most of the animals of the forest running for cover.

"Of course, I can do nothing but stand here and endure. I often wonder what it must feel like to be struck and uprooted by such force. You know they used explosives when they were building the canal and the destruction was horrible.

"I could do nothing as many of my beautiful brothers and sisters were destroyed by the builders. It had a horrible effect on me; I began to scorn humans, much as the natives had. I shut down completely and refused to communicate with humans for many years. Then you came along and rescued me from my solitude, Willie.

"I'm rambling and keeping you from sharing your story. I am sorry. Tell me of this great sea battle."

With as much theatrics as possible, I related my story of the last great sea battle of the American Revolution. In my opinion, it was another moment where David slew Goliath and the good guys prevailed.

"The American Revolution marked the end of British dominance over the Colonies and set America on the course to independence," I said. "I'm kind of proud one of the last naval battles occurred not far from here. That must have been a great day."

Of course, I had to explain to Sani how ownership of Florida had passed back and forth between the Spanish and the English, the two greatest sea-faring people of their day. She had only vague knowledge of whose flags were planted where and when. But representatives from both countries had passed beneath her welcoming canopy over the centuries.

"It's a wonderful story, Willie," Sani said. "In all of my years, only two Brits have stepped beneath these branches. I think their claim to Florida was short-lived. They seemed a bit brash to me. They killed without cause or mercy. When they left this spot, they didn't even extinguish the hot coals of their campfire. I feared a stiff wind might set the whole region ablaze.

"I also am impressed with the research you did. This library you visited must be a source of much information."

"It is a great place of learning," I replied.

"You should frequent it more often, even at the expense of coming here. We can learn much from the past, you know."

"I will never stop coming here, Sani. Our friendship and this spot among your branches has become my personal sanctuary, and I have learned much from what you have shared with me," I said. "Now, tell me of this other sea battle that was just off the shores of Flagler Beach."

"I hope I didn't mislead you. It wasn't exactly a sea battle but it did involve a would-be attack by sea and the destruction of one of the giant sailing vessels. It happened nearby, close to what you call Flagler Beach today. No large guns were fired but plenty of small arms were discharged. I learned this story from a Spanish monk who sought shelter under my branches many centuries ago. It occurred during a time possession of Florida was disputed between France and Spain.

"The French arrived on the Florida shoreline long after explorers claimed it as the property of Spain. Unlike Spain, the French didn't plant a flag and leave; they built a fort and began a settlement not far from here. They were Huguenots, seeking religious freedom, the monk told me. When news of this reached the king of [13]Spain, he was infuriated. He sent his top general to the New World to repel the infidels, as they were called by the monk. This general led a small armada to Florida's shore and founded the settlement of St. Augustine.

"Aware of the new Spanish settlement, the French decided to attack St. Augustine. But their plans and ships were scuttled by a hurricane. They were blown off course and crashed where Daytona Beach now exists. Fewer than two hundred Frenchmen survived, and they began their long trek back to their fort on foot. They had to pass through treacherous vegetation and infested swamps. Before they could find safety, the Frenchmen came face-to-face with the Spaniards at the inlet north of here. In those days, it was known as Mosquito Bay.

"Using this monk as a translator, the Spanish general encouraged the French to drop their arms and surrender. If they did not, he promised annihilation. They complied, but the Spanish general did not keep his word. He slaughtered everyone except those who proclaimed to be loyal to the Catholic Church. The Spanish opposed anyone who did not believe as they did, and proclaimed their actions fulfilled the will of their God. I don't approve of killing in any form.

"The [15]monk came here and prayed for forgiveness for his role in the massacre. He was very old and in his last days. He had left the Spanish settlement and lived among the Timucua Indians, hoping to convert their beliefs to his. It was the Timucuans who had told him my branches reached closer to his God than any other tree in the region. So, he sought my serenity as he made his final penance. [14]The monk prayed for two days and two nights. When the sun rose to brighten a third day, he took his final breath. The Timucua, being good servants of Mother Nature, took his body back to St. Augustine so he could be buried among his own people."

"Wow! You again amaze me, Sani," I replied when my friend was silent. "Did you pick all that up from the prayers of a sorrowful monk?"

"He was like you, Willie Brown, and so many before you," Sani replied. "He came here for peace and solace. He sat just below that limb you are sitting on and pressed his back against my bark. In doing so, his mind was opened to me. Anytime I didn't understand what he was saying, I just delved into his memory for an explanation. It really was a simple story of mistrust, and the monk thought for sure he would be damned for his role in it. So, he bared his soul and I listened."

"Why didn't you communicate with him, try to explain that it wasn't his fault? I would hope if I came to you with a similar problem you would help me make the right decision. That's what friends do," I pleaded.

"He really wasn't baring his soul to me, Willie," Sani explained. "He was pleading his case with his God. I only listened, as I have done throughout most of my existence."

It dawned on me at that moment how lucky I was to be able to communicate with this wonderous tree, the Queen of Flagler forests. I knew I couldn't tell anyone, though. I quickly would be labeled a lunatic. So, I pulled out 'Huck Finn' and we had a good time sharing thoughts on the first few Chapters. I skipped around some but made sure I recited most all of Mark Twain's important points.

Sani had seen the evil of men, but she was shocked a father would be so unsupportive of a son as Huck's father was of him. By the time wayward Huck was taken in by Miss Douglas, it was time for me to return home. As usual, I promised to return.

"Don't forget to bring Huck Finn with you when you return, Willie. I think the old woman is going to have a great impact on his life."

"Well, you'll have to wait and see," I replied. "There's lots of adventures ahead. I'll be back as soon as I can."

I headed home, not knowing if my story of the sea battle or Sani's recollection of the massacre at Matanzas Inlet was the most impressive. I'd been to that inlet dozens of times and never suspected its name was Spanish. I thought it was an Indian name, and I never dreamed it meant "massacre." I planned to share that little tidbit with my parents. I wanted to impress them with my reformation. I no longer was the thoughtless child who they worried about each time I ran off to the East Coast Canal. I was maturing and learning responsibility. Be certain, though. I did not plan to tell them the source of my new-found information was a tree of wonders that stood along my beloved waterway.

CHAPTER 5

I didn't get back to the canal and Sani for about a week. It was getting close to harvest time at our small farm, and my chores were increasing. I made several more stops at the Public Library. My parents noticed and approved of my sudden eagerness to study history. So, when I asked if I could camp out at the canal overnight, they approved. Mom packed me a bunch of sandwiches, some fruit and handed me the old canteen my father sometimes used when he was working out in the fields on our small farm. Dad reminded me to be careful and told me what time he expected me to return the next day.

"I want you back here by dinnertime tomorrow, and don't be late," he said. "You don't want to make your mother and me worry about you again,"

I crossed my heart, pledged obedience and off I went. I was so excited, I probably ran faster than I ever had to my most favorite place in the world. I was tucked up into Sani's branches long before the sun reached its highest point in the sky. I read Huck Finn out loud for a couple of hours before Sani said anything to me. When I got to the part where Huck meets up with Jim, the runaway slave, Sani stirred.

"Oh, I know about the plight of runaway slaves," Sani said. "More than a few have found a resting place here in the shade I offer beside these cool waters. Do you remember that Bulow Plantation attack I told you about, Willie?"

"I sure do. The Seminole Indians attacked and destroyed an old sugar plantation south of here. I remember it easily because I've visited the remains," I said.

"Well a few of the servants, the young ones who could run, escaped the carnage. Two of them stopped by here to cool down. They had been running for hours, not knowing whether the wild ones were chasing them or not. They laid down in the shallows of the creek and let the cool water bring relief to their sore muscles. Then, they both leaned up against my trunk and tried to sort out what to do next.

"These two were strong, young men. They cherished the fact they were free of the endless chores at the planation. They cut sugar cane and planted day after day, month after month, from dawn to dusk. It was hard work, but they preferred it to picking cotton.

"They pitied the savagery the inhabitants must have endured at the hands of the Seminoles. They were sorrowful for all but Big Jack, an overseer who was known to pass out punishment without mercy. Both had felt the lash at the overseer's hand. Floggings were not the worst of their existence, though. Jack had slept with almost every enslaved young woman on the plantation but gave little attention to the offspring his activities created. They became the scourge of both races, white and black."

"Those were bad times for Negroes," I replied. "I have no idea what fueled the minds of early Americans. I've read plenty about slavery in Florida and the South. I don't know how one man can hold such dominance over another and sleep at night. Those were evil times. You know that's what the Civil War was all about. The North wanted to end slavery and the South wanted to preserve it."

"Of course, I know of the Civil War. Its combatants traveled this watery highway frequently. These two travelers stopped by here long before that conflict, though." Sani explained.

"I'm sorry. I didn't mean to interrupt you, Sani. Please continue," I said.

"They were a hardy pair, or they wouldn't have been able to escape the Seminoles. They were scared and excited about escaping bondage. They sat here and debated whether to head north to Charleston, where the Bulow family originated, or flee to the Everglades where it was rumored other slaves lived freely."

"I sure hope they decided the swamp was their only salvation. I can't imagine how two escaped slaves could make it on foot through Georgia and the Carolinas to get to Charleston, in those days," I said. "They surely would have been caught and probably hung for running away."

"They chose the Everglades, Willie, but it was not an easy decision. All they had was the clothes on their backs, and it wasn't in the greatest condition. They had no food and they had to travel over territory that was unfamiliar and foreboding. They were wise enough to know the sun rose in the east and set in the west, assuring them which direction was south."

Again, I marveled at the knowledge Sani possessed, simply by the fact she had stood on this Flagler ground for so many centuries. Her

33

ability to extract information from passersby and her recall was amazing. She taught me the value of listening. It was a lesson worth heeding, one I have practiced throughout my adult life.

I wanted to know more about the relationship between the blacks and the Seminoles, though. I knew from my research the Seminole tribe was a composite of many native tribes from the north. It stands to reason they would welcome former slaves and freed men into their society.

Often when the Seminoles raided a plantation, they would let the slaves go free because they were aware of their oppression. [16]The Black Seminoles were made up of free blacks and runaway slaves who joined forces with the Seminole Indians in Florida from approximately 1700 through the 1850s. Their numbers grew steadily, and they were celebrated for their bravery and tenacity during all three Seminole Wars.

"Did the Bulow survivors mention anything about willingly joining the Seminole tribe?" I asked. "Florida offered easy entry for runaway slaves and freedmen who wanted to escape the oppression of Georgia, Alabama and other southern states."

Sani paused before answering, as if she was searching her memory, and then admitted: "Few Black Seminoles have crossed beneath my branches. Of course, I sense things because I cannot see as you humans do," Sani explained. "Now that you mention it, I do remember a short discussion about going back to the Bulow Plantation and tracking the savages to their village. These two lads believed the Indians might have taken several young women as hostages. I can only presume they would have assimilated into the Seminole society. Despite their savagery, the Seminoles cherished family, and the black women would have found a better existence among the natives than their white overseers."

"Sani, you have turned me into a history fanatic," I confessed. "I so appreciate you sharing your stories with me. I find I'm spending more and more time at the library in search of little known facts about Flagler County."

"I'm equally enjoying the story of Huckleberry Finn, Willie. Will you tell me more about their journey down the Mississippi River?"

34

"I've got good news, Sani," I replied. "I have my parents' permission to camp here by the East Coast Canal for the night. I must return home tomorrow, but I won't be grounded for spending a night in your branches this time. I'll read you all about Huck and Jim's journey down the Mississippi."

"I am pleased to hear that, but I must inquire if you have disclosed our friendship to your parents?"

"Oh, no! Everyone back home knows I love to come here, but they don't know any details. It's a secret that must remain between us."

"I think that is wise, Willie Brown. Would you read to me for a little while before the forest grows dark?"

"Absolutely!"

I think Sani liked listening to the misadventures of Huck as much as I enjoyed reading them over and over. The Mississippi was not so much different than the East Coast Canal that flowed nearby. They both provided endless opportunities for someone to travel from one place to another. The Mississippi, because of its size and the many towns that grew up on its banks, provided a highway between destinations. So, did the canal, which in its earliest development, provided a smooth passage from Jacksonville down the eastern coastline of the peninsula. Today, Floridians can motor all the way from Jacksonville to Miami on the Intracoastal Waterway.

Huck and Jim's encounters with hoodlums, thieves, liars and murderers surprised Sani. She didn't know such criminal activity ran rampant in the human world. But she was familiar with the fog that allowed the rafters to paddle right by their Cairo destination. She also could relate to the times the pair floated smoothly down the river under a harsh sun. The similarities helped her easily understand the story as it unfolded.

By the time darkness set in, I had eaten a couple of sandwiches and an orange. I again began asking Sani questions about the past.

"Did the survivors of the Bulow Plantation raid ever return to this part of the country, Sani?" I asked.

"I don't think so," she replied. "I like to think they blended into the Florida population and became productive citizens. They certainly had to be resourceful to escape and get this far. Florida, at that time, was a rugged wilderness that could gobble up anyone or anything that did not show it respect and care."

"I can't imagine what life was like back in those days," I stated. "Florida's early settlers had to be made of pretty good stuff to survive the climate and environment."

"I think the black men, as you call them, were well-suited for the challenge. Their bodies were strong and hard from years and years of back-breaking labor on the plantations that once dominated this region. The two who stopped here had spent their entire lives in captivity. They knew nothing other than slavery.

"Years later, black cowboys stopped here to water their horses, gather food and rest from their travels. These old branches have never failed to provide a respite for weary travelers."

"Black cowboys?" I asked.

"Yes, what about them?" Sani replied.

"I've never heard of such a thing. Most the cowboys I've seen or read about were white men who rode dusty trails out west. I didn't know there were cowboys in Florida."

"Sure! Lots of [18]cattle, horses and cows, ran wild throughout this region, and cowboys came here to gather them up. When the Spanish came to Florida, they brought with them a variety of four-legged creatures that were not natural to this land. Initially, the settlers raised cattle to feed the growing settlement. The Spanish let their cattle roam freely, finding food and water wherever they could. So, they multiplied naturally and grew in numbers.

"Those early settlers were experts whip handlers. One bragged to his partners about his accuracy. He snapped the head off a copperhead snake with one flick of his wrist and bragged about it. There was three of them here at the time, and they all raved about the precision strike. I felt sorry for the snake, but he should have known better than to show himself in the daylight with humans around."

"It seems Florida helped former slaves evolve, and we seldom hear anything about it. They went from being flogged by cruel masters to wielding whips of their own with deadly accuracy," I observed out loud.

Nonetheless, I knew Florida was a slave state for many years, even joining the Confederacy. It made me feel good the survivors and runaways were able to carve out new lives in the wilderness. It was a testament to their determination and their strength of character. Sani agreed.

"These Florida cattlemen were called [18]Crackers because of their skilled handling of the whips they used to roundup steers. And they came in all sizes and colors," she added. "They weren't all just runaway slaves. Florida had a very diverse beginning. White settlers sought the wild cows and horses left behind by the Spanish just as much as the freedmen and the native people. This was a logical place to find all kinds of domestic animals. They came to feed in the hammocks and grasslands of the region and enjoy the water that flowed freely. Those the alligators didn't consume were rounded up by the Crackers and taken to ranches all across the state.

"The Crackers conducted regular roundups of the four-legged beasts, a tedious chore being they had no idea where to find the free-roaming critters. Quite often they had several steers already collected when they stopped here. It was a great place to camp, as you well know. Then almost always they drove the animals south to where larger ranchers payed them for their efforts.

"The Cow Hunters were a tough breed of men. They often showed up here after months on the trail. They almost always took advantage of the fresh water to bathe and clean their equipment. When they came in groups, inevitably one would sit in my branches and watch for rustlers while the others went about their chores or slept.

"Rustlers were everywhere. More than once, a lookout has fired a weapon from high up in my branches to scare thieves away. In all my years, only one rustler was brave enough to shoot back. If you climb almost to the top of my crown, you might be able to see where the bullet is still lodged."

"Oh my, that must have been painful," I said.

"Yes, but my healing sap works extremely fast within my system. The pain subsided quickly. I was happy when that bunch of Crackers left this region the next morning. I will not complain about them because they were a considerate bunch. They always put out their fires and cleaned up after themselves.

"The one who sat in my branches as lookout seemed honest. His thoughts always centered on his family. In fact, all the Crackers did.

They all had wives and children waiting for them somewhere south of here.

"Some of the same fellows stopped back here many years later as part of the [19] Cow Cavalry that supplied food for the Confederate Army The same young man who had climbed my branches to fulfill his role as lookout climbed up again.," Sani said.

"How were you able to recognize him?" I asked.

"Every species, especially humans, has a unique imprint. I could tell it was him the minute his hand touched my bark. His name was Nathaniel Youngblood. He was much older on his second trip to this region.

"Frankly, Nathaniel was scared to death and had mixed emotions about helping the Confederate effort. However, Florida had been good to him and he wanted to respectfully do his part as payment for his freedom. Twenty years had passed since he escaped the shackles of slavery and Florida was the land he loved and the home of his growing family. He climbed up in my branches because it was safer than being on the ground. He could see the enemy coming and rarely could they see him.

"The Cow Cavalry had to be on the alert constantly because the Unionists would do anything to break that supply train. It was an arduous task herding cattle from Florida to Savannah and Charleston. There were few outfits that made the trek unscathed.

"Unlike you, Willie, Nathaniel had a hard time sleeping because he had been shot at several times. Every sound in the forest made him jump. When he did sleep, I tried to drop some extra leaves onto his chest, hoping they would allow him to rest a little more peacefully. I don't think it ever worked, though.

"The Civil War years were tumultuous for everyone, because the Cow Calvary was driving supplies north every week. The only time Nathaniel stopped here was when he was heading north. I never learned if his outfit made their delivery successfully or not. And I've often wondered if he made it back to his family."

"Tell you what I'll do Sani," I said. "The next time I go to the library, I'll see if I can track down his name. I'm sure there is a registry of Floridians who served in the Civil War. Our public library is packed full of stuff like that."

"I'd appreciate it, Willie. Your library sounds like a wonderful place. Why are you spending so much time here when you could be absorbing knowledge there?"

"Because the things I learn from you can't be discovered in a library, Sani. I've just never met someone who could entertain and educate as well as you. Of course, I love your branches and the surrounding countryside, too. This is my home away from home."

"Thank you, Willie. That is probably the nicest compliment anyone has ever given me. Of course, I haven't communicated with anyone for several centuries. I'm glad you keep coming back. I enjoy your company. "

I spent the rest of the night answering question from Sani. She wanted to know about my family, my school and my friends. I opened up like a hymnal on Sunday morning. It was well past midnight when I fell asleep on that big branch and my back snuggled comfortably against Sani's warm bark.

CHAPTER 6

The coolness of the night had no effect on me. Sani could use her sap to generate heat whenever my body touched her bark. She made sure I was comfortable during my overnighter. One thing you learn by spending time in the wild is the fact Mother Nature wakes up long before the sun scorches the horizon. The finches, robins and warblers provided a wonderful symphony as the crickets and frogs went into hiding. I could hear the kingfish and pelican calling their mates from the nearby shores of the Atlantic Ocean, too. It was an unforgettable concerto, one I still cherish today. Many times I find myself waking before dawn, just so I can listen to the changing of nature's guard.

I pulled out my last sandwich and ate it after taking care of my morning business. My canteen was still half full of water and it was cool and refreshing. Then, I climbed back up into Sani's branches and read Huckleberry Finn most of the morning. We were getting toward the end when I started getting tired and redirect our conversation. A couple conmen had led Huck astray and forced he and Tom Sawyer to jump on a raft and escape down the river once again. They were sorrowful times for Huck. Jim had been sold back into slavery and the boys were about to plan his rescue. The drama got me to thinking about all the trials and tribulations settlers endured when they ventured into Florida's vast wilderness, and I asked Sani about it.

"Being this was a waterway of considerable length before the canal was constructed, how did most early settlers pass through here?" I asked. "We take travel through Florida and other parts of country for granted because there are paved highways leading us everywhere. There were no highways for the settlers to follow. I know you said they followed the streams and game trails. How frequently did settlers pass right through this little clearing?"

"Before the canal was built, the only way to get from St. Augustine to here was by boat or The King's Road, west of here," Sani explained. "There were rafts, similar to the one Huck and Jim took down the Mississippi, canoes and flatboats that traveled up and down the waterway in those days. Eventually, once the canal was complete, bigger boats and steamships began to disturb the peace with their billowing smoke and noisy engines.

"Initially, though, travel was slow and difficult, winding from creeks to lakes to rivers and eventually to St. Augustine. But the procession was constant. Settlers were always looking for farmland and high country where they could begin new lives. They also passed this way on horseback, by wagon and on the strength of their own two legs. I'm sure there have been thousands who have passed me on foot and walked the length of this state.

"Similarly, many more traveled [20]The King's Road but it was treacherous, I was told. Settlers were easily attacked by Indians and men of little character. Many were ragged and desperate after living months in the wilderness. Unsuspecting settlers often were assaulted, robbed and even murdered.

"I felt sorry for the early settlers. They had no idea what they were in for when they crossed the Georgia line and set foot in Florida. You cannot comprehend how difficult conditions could be back then. Water was everywhere and so, too, were the insects, snakes and other unfriendly creatures. In the summer, the heat was oppressive. When winter arrived, sometimes the cold gusts coming off the ocean were bitter enough to chase most of the wildlife inland. It was not unusual for most of the natural fauna of the area to freeze and perish as ice covered every surface in this small clearing. Twice the creek that flowed freely through here froze solid, along with many of the living creatures it supported.

"Humans, in their flimsy lean-tos and shacks, had no way to survive. There wasn't enough lumber in the area to support warming fires twenty-four hours a day, sometimes for weeks. They either froze to death or packed up their things and moved south where warmer temperatures made survival easier.

"Those who stayed, fought off all kinds of calamities. I can't tell you how many times frantic fathers and tearful mothers bathed their children in that creek, trying to arrest the [21]fever that seemed to come from nowhere when they crossed into this low country.

"This also was the spot where many animals of the region came to eat and drink. Do you remember me telling you how plentiful the fish were in this creek?"

"Yes," I replied. "You said the young children of the Timucua used to race across the river, stepping on the backs of the fish and barely getting wet. I would have given anything to see a stream so bountiful with marine life today. It would never happen, though. Too many of today's sportsmen are not conservationists; they would have pulled every last fish from your stream in a very short time. It's why so many species are extinct today. Look what they did to the buffalo out west."

"I don't believe I know of buffalo, Willie."

"Ah, this is a good morning, Sani. You get to learn from me," I said with light-heartedness in my tone.

"It is always good when you and I are sharing stories, Willie. In all of my years, I don't know if I have enjoyed another human as much as I enjoy you. I am happy you feel the same way," my friend said warmly.

"A buffalo can best be described as a cross between a bull and the largest bear. They have horns, four legs and they can weigh as much as two thousand pounds. Do you understand weight, Sani?" I asked.

"I can imagine it," she replied. "because lumbermen talked about loading lumber by the ton onto barges to be shipped north to St. Augustine when that city was coming of age. A ton was a lot of lumber. They cut lumber all around here. I was lucky they did not touch me with their axes and saws or we would not be communicating today."

"I'm glad they didn't either," I said. "Nobody had better ever try to remove you from this site. I won't let anything like that happen to you as long as I'm around," I confessed.

"Thank you, Willie."

"Let me get back to my buffalo story, though," I explained. "Buffalo roamed the plains of the West by the millions. They wandered the plains in large herds. Historians say some herds stretched across five square miles and, when they began to run, the earth shook as if the ground was going to open in a great seizure.

"The buffalo was cherished by the Native Americans for the large amount of food they provided, as well as their skin. It was a thick leather with lots of hair. They were used as coats and blankets to fend off the cold winter weather. It was those coats and hats that brought about their sudden demise. Once they were introduced on the East Coast, all of America wanted winter gear made from the buffalo's hide. The price of the hides skyrocketed.

"So, large groups of hunters raided the plains and massacred the buffalo for just their skins. Quite often, they took their skin and left the carcasses to rot in the prairie. They hunted the buffalo almost to extinction."

"What a waste that must have been," Sani said, sounding sorrowful. "It is no surprise the native people of this land resented the white man so. He took without asking and left terrible consequences behind. I think thoughtlessness and indifference is inherent to your species. Humans seldom respect Mother Nature."

"Yes, but sometimes Mother Nature fights back. I think you were about to tell me how this harsh landscape reacted to the intrusion of settlers," I countered.

"I think the early settlers were harassed most by the insects. They called this area Mosquito County for a reason. The pests attacked in huge swarms and infected many with deadly fevers, especially the children of the families who passed by here. They were defenseless against the insects. They tried everything to keep them away, from setting blazing fires at night to packing their skin with swamp mud to keep them from biting during the day. I cannot tell you how many mothers wrapped their children in cloths to keep the insects away. Others had no other choice but to place their children's beds by their campfires and spend the entire night fanning the sleeping youngsters to keep the insects at bay. At the same time, they had to cover their own face and nose with cloths to keep from inhaling the swarming pests. The mosquitoes were relentless.

"But so were the alligators, bears and big cats. The cats would wait for the adults to wander off and then snatch a child and carry it off into the wild. The alligators did the same thing, but often they attacked from the water. The bear did not care. He destroyed anything that got between him and his next meal. The bear loved the fish of this stream and had been feeding here long before the Indians or the white man happened by. They didn't like the settlers any more than the Seminoles did; they feasted on human flesh frequently.

"The settlers often carried weapons, but few were powerful enough to stop a charging bear. Like you say, they often are mammoth, much like the buffalo you told me about. When they struck a blow for

Mother Nature, it was swift and violent. The bear was, and is today, the mightiest of nature's predators."

"Travel must have been extremely difficult through here. I can't imagine what it must have been like when children were involved. Anyone who dared to venture to this land had to be made of hardy stock just to survive. Did most of the settlers bring children along?" I asked.

"The [22]Spanish who came to this land so many years ago, brought their families with them from their homeland. Occasionally, young men and boys would come this way hunting or fishing with their fathers. Living in St. Augustine, I think, better prepared them for excursions to this region. Of course, most of the Spanish wore better clothing. The settlers who came here from the north had been on the trail for months. Most of their clothing was worn and ragged.

"The Spanish children were fun-loving. They generally searched the creek bed for shiny pebbles, shells and stones that they took back to their homes. They were used for games of entertainment. They often played their games under my branches while their fathers fished or skinned the animals they had harvested. Spanish women never joined in the hunt. It was a long time before a female enjoyed the shade of my leafy branches.

"The wives, sisters and daughters of the settlers suffered greatly in the oppressive heat and harshness of the land. I remember one sorrowful day a young woman staggered up the trail from Long's Creek and sought refuge beneath my limbs. She was heavy with child and starving. She was alone when I felt her lean against me for support. She had been wounded in an Indian attack and her life was fading. She was praying to her God as she took her last breath. The last thing she did was deliver her baby in the shade of my canopy. Neither of them survived.

"She was found by the Seminoles whose arrow most likely caused her death. As vicious as they could be, the Seminoles cherished motherhood. I'm sure they took both bodies and disposed of them in a ritual that brought honor to both mother and child. It was a very sad day, because I felt both of their lives slip away," Sani said.

Sani's story horrified me. Murder and mayhem were not unknown to me. I had read plenty of Louis L'Amore novels of the Wild West, and the legends of Daniel Boone and Davy Crockett were more than familiar. When I was a young boy, I had my own "coonskin hat" to emulate my heroes. Sani's tales of Florida's early settlers were not make-believe; they were a revelation of a life in a harsh and unforgiving land.

"That is horrible!" I said after much thought. "Life here must have been so difficult. I don't think I would have liked to be part of a family that traveled to this untamed land prior to the twentieth century. It was a massive undertaking and filled with pain. Did any of the families stay along this trail for any amount of time?"

"No, as you know, the land in this region is very low and susceptible to flooding, especially before this canal was built. There was one small family that made a temporary camp about a stone's throw from here. In a very short time, the adult male made a respectable shelter for his wife and two children who were gravely ill. He stuck large limbs in the ground and then wove smaller, pliable saplings through the mainstays to create walls of a kind. He stuffed mud and moss between the saplings to keep the bugs and inclement weather out. He used the large palmettos and palm fronds to craft a thatched roof.

"It provided safe haven as his family recuperated. I helped a little in that matter. He was exhausted one day when he came to rest in the shade. He quickly fell asleep, leaning against me for support. I planted the thought in his mind that if he boiled my leaves in water it might bring relief to his ailing family. When he awoke he got right to it, even though his wife raved about the bitter taste. In a week, they were well enough to continue their journey. "

"You are amazing, Sani. I hope that family made it to wherever they were heading," I said.

"Me too. They took lots of my leaves with them and had several jugs they filled with my tea before departing. I think it is important for Mother Nature to show kindness when all about seems hopeless."

"You certainly have shown me nothing but kindness, Sani. I like to think Mother Nature is looking down at us and smiling."

"Oh, I am sure she is, Willie," Sani said. "But time is waning. Would you mind reading a few more Chapters of Huck Finn before you have to be on your way?"

"I think that is a good idea," I replied. "There are some parts coming up I think you will like. I want to share them with you before I have to leave. I cannot be late, being my parents were kind enough to allow me to spend the night."

"You are wise beyond your years, Willie, and I'd love to hear what happens next for Huck Finn, Tom Sawyer and Jim."

Sani listened intently as Tom and Huck concocted a hair-brained plan to free Jim once again. In doing so, they tormented Jim's captors and reverted to their old thieving ways. By the time I got to Chapter 39, the sun was beginning to sink in the sky, and I had to return home. I climbed down from Sani's branches, bid her farewell and let the ocean breeze hit my back as I ran toward civilization.

"I'll be back in a couple of days," I promised as I ran toward the trail the led to my parents' home.

CHAPTER 7

I learned more about Flagler County history from Sani that summer than I had in all my years. More importantly, she lit a spark in me and sent me on a quest to learn as much as I could about my home. Whenever my parents when into town, I had them drop me off at the Public Library.

I think I took after my mother. She was an avid reader, and I have fond memories of her reading to me when I was very young. So, I grew up with a love for books. I read everything I could get my hands on, including many of the classics. Of course, Edgar Rice Burroughs was one of my favorites, along with Dickens, Twain and L'Amore.

On my last visit before the school year renewed, I finished reading "The Adventures of Huckleberry Finn." We discussed at length what life must have been in those days adrift on the largest river in North America. Sani had no way of knowing about human senses such as desperation, love, hate or suffering other than what she had gleaned from the people who passed by the clearing where she stood. I like to think she had gained a stronger sense of human life by connecting with me and, of course, the deranged Captain Ahab and mischievous Huckleberry Finn.

At long last, our discussion turned to the East Coast Canal and its construction. As usual, I did some research before approaching the topic with her. I knew the section that was constructed through Flagler County was the most difficult of the entire waterway. It had been debated and legislated over and over. It took almost a century before the first eighteen-mile leg of it was completed.

Thanks to my many excursions to the library, I discovered a four-mile, 36 feet wide canal had been completed from the [23]Matanzas River to Mala Compra Creek by 1883. What lay south was a savanna, three-quarters of a mile long, followed by half-mile of hammock and two miles of sand flats, coquina rock, cabbage palms and palmettos before reaching the marshes of Smith Creek. Smith Creek provided a straight shot to the Halifax River.

It wasn't until May 13, 1907, at 8 o'clock in the morning, the waters of the Matanzas Bay and the Halifax Rivers were finally joined. The final obstruction was removed by the dredge boat *South Carolina*, bringing the project to a close. Needless to say, the massive flow of water was refreshing for Sani.

"One of the reasons I have been able to survive for all these years is because of the abundance of water in this region," Sani explained. "My root system runs far and deep and it absorbs huge quantities of water. Why do you think my leaves stay so beautifully green all year, Willie?"

"I'm guessing because you get lots to drink," I replied.

"I'm no different than any other of Mother Nature's creatures," she explained. "We all need water to survive. Much of what I consume, I release into the air and it helps create this rich environment that constantly regenerates itself on either side of the waterway.

"The waterway was not always this large. For most of my life I drew my water from a sizeable creek that ran through here. It was fed by the Matanzas River to the north and natural springs along the way. In all my time, I have seen it slow to a trickle only once. For most of my days, the creek was large enough to support small boats and canoes, and it always was teaming with fish and other aquatic species."

More than a century ago, I explained to Sani, Congress recognized the need for transportation, aside from the often hazardous passages by the large ships that sailed up and down the Atlantic Coast. Along with costly fares, bad weather and treacherous currents, pirates patrolled the southern coastlines and preyed on passenger vessels.

"More than one of those evil privateers, as they liked to be called, sought shelter under my branches," Sani confirmed. "Most of them were as wicked as the darkest clouds that sometimes roll inland from the Atlantic Ocean."

"Wow! I didn't know pirates landed in this area," I replied. "Did you ever come across Blackbeard or Calico Jack? They were famous pirates who were known to scavenge the Atlantic and Caribbean waters."

"I don't recall hearing those names," she replied. "Most of the scoundrels who came this way were marooners."

"What's a marooner?" I asked immediately.

"They were the worst of the worst; [24]pirates who were put ashore because their actions aboard the large sailing vessels no longer could be tolerated. They were simply thrown overboard and cast away.

"Most of the men who stopped here were close to death from starvation or exposure to the elements. One died while leaning against my trunk and then was drug off by an alligator. I didn't feel sorry for him, because he spent most of his last days ranting and raving about revenge. He might have been the most miserable human I have encountered. I was quick to let my reptile friends know there was fresh meat nearby, and glad when he was gone."

"Are you saying you summoned an alligator to drag his body away?" I asked.

"Of course, Willie. Don't be shocked. Life and death occur daily along the shores of this waterway. It is nature's way of nourishing itself."

"Of course, you are right," I replied. "The graphic picture of a gator dragging a body off into the wilds gives me the creeps, though."

"I'm sorry, Willie, but I'm happy to tell you not all of the marooners met such a horrible fate. Another cast-off and privateer, named Malachi, strolled this way one summer long ago and survived for a month before he just wandered off and never returned. I don't know if he signaled a passing ship or found safe haven elsewhere."

"How did he survive in the wilderness for a month?" I asked.

"His timing was perfect, because he arrived just before the turtles began their annual nesting along the coastline," Sani said.

"I've seen their nests," I replied. "My father and I camped on the shore once when one of those nests came to life. It was amazing. There must have been dozens of those tiny babies trying to make it back to the sea. I had never seen anything quite like it."

"I imagine it was," Sani replied. "The nests are not as plentiful as they once were, though. Long ago, the sea turtles used to come ashore in huge masses to make their nests and fill them with eggs.

"The [25]moon was full when the sound of the Loggerheads' flippers scraping against the sand and seashells awakened Malachi from a sound sleep. He was so scared by the sound, he climbed up into my branches for fear some sea creature was coming ashore in search of a human meal.

"The next morning, he found the nests and returned with his shirt sleeves and pantlegs filled with tiny turtle eggs. He cooked them over a fire and feasted for several days. One day he left to retrieve more eggs and never returned."

"What happened to him?" I asked.

"I don't know, but I would guess Mother Nature paid him back for his theft of the eggs."

"How?"

"As I have told you, all species have a way of communicating, Willie. Just as I know when a hurricane approaches this shore or the time has come for the black bear to go into hibernation, I know when nesting season approaches. So do many other creatures. Bears and raccoons, snakes and lizards, spiders and crabs all know, too. They also feed on the eggs. A Loggerhead lays them by the hundreds.

"My guess is that Malachi interrupted the feast of one of the forest's larger creatures and paid the ultimate price. Whatever was his fate, I was glad to see him gone. He had no respect for me or the land. He was the first human to attack my branches with a ferociousness that was painful."

"Did he try to chop you down?" I asked.

"No, but he stupidly severed many of my branches to burn in his fire. His knowledge of the sea did not teach him dry, dead wood burns better than freshly-cut oak."

"I am sorry he treated you so poorly," I replied. "I have no idea why anyone would want to cut you into pieces or remove you from this landscape. Your beauty is unmatched by anything else within my view."

"Thank you, Willie, I appreciate your kind words," Sani replied. "Malachi was not the first nor the last human who looked at me with destruction in their eye. I almost fell to the laborer's ax when they were building this canal you so love."

"Really? I can't imagine what that was like. Can you tell me about it, the building of the canal, I mean?"

"I'd be glad to, but first you must read me another of your Superman comics. Your Man of Steel is so interesting, I never knew such humans existed," Sani said.

"Today is your lucky day Sani," I said. "My father brought home a new one just last night. It's entitled "The Last Days of Superman," and it appears something or someone is killing our hero."

"No, I thought he was indestructible!" Sani said, startled.

"Don't forget, he is weakened to near death when exposed to Kryptonite," I replied.

"Oh, stop teasing me, Willie. Climb up here and read it to me. I've got to know what happens to the Man of Steel. "

I didn't realize I had turned Sani into such a Superman fan, but this new revelation made me tease her even more.

"I thought I might drop a line in the water first, if you don't mind. I think I saw a drum jump right over there next to those rocks. My parents would be tickled pink if I brought it home for supper."

"Oh, if you must. Why can't you fish from my branches and read at the same time?"

"You're asking a lot of me," I replied. "I'm just a kid. If I try to do too many things at once, I might fall."

"You're being silly, Willie. You know I'd never let you fall from any of my limbs."

Anxious to read the story myself, I relented with laughter. "All right. I can't wait any longer myself. I'll be right up."

I climbed faster than [26]Jack scrambled up the beanstalk. I don't know why I felt so much comfort sitting on the big limbs of that Live Oak. With my legs stretched across a limb that was as big around as me and my back pressed firmly against Sani's warm trunk, I couldn't have been more comfortable if I had been in my own mama's embrace.

Sani said it was the sap that ran through every molecule in her structure that created our bond, but I think there was more to it than that. To this day, I haven't been able to resurrect the spiritual nature of our connection. It was simply amazing.

CHAPTER 8

[27]"The Last Days of Superman" was everything I had hoped it would be. For a dreamy kid like me, who spent hours talking to a daggum tree, it sent my imagination soaring. Sani liked it, too. I swear I heard her gasp a couple of times when death seemed imminent.

I can remember the storyline as if I was reading it today, and I'm going to tell it to you whether you want to read it or not. It's a heap more interesting that "Moby Dick." I promise. If you don't like it, turn the page and we'll get on with the business of how the East Coast Canal almost brought down Sani's ancient limbs for good.

Or you can read about one of the most harrowing moments in Superman's career, and you know he had a lot of those. I'll try and keep it short and sweet:

Superman comes in contact with Virus X, deadly for anyone from the planet Krypton, while pushing a spiraling satellite away from the unknowing citizens of Metropolis.

The exposure weakens Superman to the point he must retreat to his Fortress of Solitude and ponder all he has accomplished since arriving on Earth, as well as the things he has not. The Man of Steel goes to the Daily Planet and announces he has one more task to complete before he succumbs to Virus X. He is going to build a series of canals around Earth as part of a complex irrigation system. He is too weak to complete it, though, and he calls on Supergirl, Krypto and the Legion of Super-Heroes to carry on his final task. With their aid, he manages to build the irrigation system and his friends complete a long list of other tasks. They pulverize a rogue comet, destroy some space fungus and create an artificial moon over Antarctica as time runs out for Superman.

With his friend Jimmy Olsen constantly at his side, Superman decides to use the last of his power to reveal his true identity to the world by etching it on the surface of the moon with his laser-like vision.

Saturn Girl saves the day when she discovers Kryptonite –
lodged in Jimmy's camera — is poisoning Superman and not
Virus X. Once removed, the Man of Steel returns to full
health, and Supergirl and Krypto use their x-ray vision to
erase the message from the surface of the moon.

The Legion of Super-Heroes returns to their own time and
Superman goes on to make comic book history.

Both Sani and I were mesmerized by the story. For a young boy, Superman was an easy hero and the writers kept us guessing the outcome right up to the end. I read it twice, front to back. Me and Sani hung on every word.

Superman debuted in the late 1930s, the brainchild of two Cleveland (Ohio) Glenville High School students, Jerry Siegel and Joe Shuster. They sold their rights to the characters to DC comics for peanuts, and the rest is history. The timing for Superman was perfect. He caught the imagination of a society that was caught in the economic squeeze of The Great Depression. Clark Kent and Superman gave the American people hope. During World War II, the Man of Steel even chipped in and helped the Allies fight off the evil Nazi and Japanese war machines.

The two original creators never really benefitted from the Superman phenomena. After a series of lawsuits, Warner Communications (the parent company of DC Comics) granted the pair a lifetime pension of $20,000 a year. They later increased it to $30,000, plus health benefits.

Years later, I read Superman comics to my children. It wasn't long after that Christopher Reeve made Superman even more famous when he stepped from a phone booth onto the silver screen with an "S" emblazed on his chest.

Before the Man of Steel became a world-wide hit, I was struck by the impact words — even those in a trivial comic book — can have on readers. If a writer can get the right words in the right place at the right time, they can transcend generations. It's one of the major motivators pushing me to reveal the story of my childhood friend, Sani. And I'm sure hoping you are enjoying it.

As for the day in question, it slipped away quickly as Sani and I bantered about the wonders of Superman and all of his friends. She never got a chance to tell me how the building of the East Coast Canal almost brought an end to her long standing in Flagler County, but she promised to tell me the next time I came to visit.

* * *

I RETURNED IN a couple of days and was eager to hear more about the construction of my beloved [28]East Coast Canal. I had spent several hours at the Public Library trying to learn more about it on my own. So, I looked forward to hearing the intimate details only Sani could relate.

I knew the waterway had been debated by lawmakers for decades. Flatboats, canoes and rafts could travel from the north side of Mosquito County to St. Augustine through a series of waterways but the trip was arduous.

Early settlers generally began their northward trip from a wharf at Long's Landing, just east of the present day Palm Coast Yacht Club. Travelers followed Long's Creek to where it met with the Matanzas River, near Washington Oaks State Park. Then they would have to cross the Matanzas Inlet to the mouth of the St. Johns River and sail on into the ancient city.

From the south, travelers would take the Halifax River into Mosquito County, but it stopped about three miles south of present-day High Bridge. The Halifax took them to Smith Creek, but then travelers had to navigate jungle-like marshlands in order to get to Long's Landing, Making construction through the heart of Mosquito County (now Flagler) mandatory.

Once work began in 1881, the Flagler portion of the canal was some of the most difficult because it was abject wilderness. That meant engineers had to find a way to connect the Matanzas and Halifax Rivers over infested marshlands and rolling hammocks to create a thoroughfare that would support heavy transportation.

The work was back-breaking, Sani confirmed. Besides dredging for a waterway that was to be five feet deep and fifty feet wide, trees and jungle-like plant growth of all kinds had to be removed. Often, explosives were used when [29]coquina rock deposits blocked dredging operations.

Sani said the explosives that destroyed most of her family, also drove away much of the wildlife. All that remained in the area were the big cats, panthers and jaguars.

"They are cunning creatures," Sani explained. "Florida panthers are large and they ruled this wild country for centuries. The region was teaming with the foods they needed to survive. Their quickness allowed them to sneak up on large birds, and they raided many of the turtle nests. Their favorite prey was the small alligators which were far more plentiful before civilization encroached on these lands. I think the cats saw the sudden influx of humans working on the canal as a source of food. So, they stayed and stalked the human laborers, even though they weren't as defenseless as the birds and alligators."

I interrupted Sani and informed her the Florida panther was now listed as an endangered species. "Humans are a lot more aware of the importance of Mother Nature's creatures," I said. "The buffalo are surging back in great numbers and the government has made it illegal to hunt the Florida panther, sea turtles and the black bear, to name just a few."

"That is good news," she replied, "because the canal workers who came here in waves destroyed everything in their path. Of course, they were preceded by surveyors and engineers and then more surveyors. Most all of them stopped to soak up some shade under my branches. They couldn't decide exactly where the canal should go. It was important to follow the natural waterway, but they had to clear huge masses of land to make it happen.

"One group came through and marked the trees that were to be removed. My timber was coveted and marked for removal, along with almost every one of my species that existed in this area.

"I was lucky because one of the chief engineers was familiar with this section of the creek and was outraged when he saw I was targeted for removal. His name was George Bradley, and he had spent many hours studying maps beneath my branches. He called every worker in his crew to my location and warned if any man laid an ax or a saw to my trunk, the punishment would be so severe they would wish they had died in the quicksand they found just north of here. He drove a nail into my side that supported a notice of protection for me.

"A conservationist and builder, Bradley continued to use my shade for meetings with his workers but moved on as work on this part of the project was abandoned. The reason I stand today is a credit to none other than [30]George Bradley."

"Did you ever get a chance to thank him?" I asked, assuming Sani might have revealed herself to one of her most important supporters.

"I did not, Willie," she replied. "You must understand I was spared by his order, but it was he who ordered the destruction of many of my brethren. It was a time of great sorrow for me."

"I understand. That must have been a difficult time," I said warmly. "How many of your family did they cut down, Sani?"

"Look around," she said. "There are only about a dozen of us still standing in this location. Before the canal, my species lined the creek for as far as the eye could see. For what it is worth, we did not make it easy on the lumbermen. Our fibers are hard. Many blades were broken before my brethren disappeared. There were many injuries and a couple deaths, too, before the area was cleared.

"The men grumbled about it every day, because they came here on the lunch breaks in order to get out of the baking and relentless sun. I was happy to spread my limbs as wide as possible to accommodate them. Of course, they also helped keep me informed about what was going on all around me, too.

"They all complained about the strenuous work. More than one of the men succumbed to heat stroke, even though they carted large containers of water here from St. Augustine daily. They parked them near here and erected a tent to provide medical care for the workers.

"Frankly, I don't know how any of those workers got any sleep at night. The sounds that came from that medical tent were frightening. I'll bet they echoed all the way to the Atlantic shoreline."

"Why was that, Sani?" I asked.

"Some of the men became delirious in the throes of fever caused by the constant attacks of insects. Sometimes the swarms of mosquitoes were so great the men wore masks to keep from ingesting them. The engineers surrounded their heads in netting to keep the pests away. There were times, the workers had to completely cover their bodies with clothing to fend off the endless biting.

"Many workers lost limbs as a result of snake bites or injuries from sharp instruments. They were transported to the medical tent, where they cried and screamed until they died or passed out from their misery.

"One giant of a man died right below where you now sit, Willie. He had stepped into a nest of tiny rattlers and was bitten several times. He refused amputation and requested he be placed at my side so he could die in the shade. As the end came near, he started to sing in the deepest, most rhythmic voice. I could feel his pain disappear as his voice reverberated through my foliage. It wasn't long before all the work crews were singing with him. When his voice faded to silence and I could no longer sense a heartbeat, they all came by and paid their respects to Rufus. I have no idea where they buried him, but it took six men to carry him off."

I cringed at the thought of stepping into a nest of snakes, especially those pigmy rattlers that seemed to be everywhere in this part of Florida. Today anti-venom to combat their poison is not readily available, and it is very expensive. In the nineteenth century, quick amputation was the only solution to stop the flow of poison.

I asked Sani how long the men worked in this area before the waterflow increased, but she couldn't tell me. She said the work crews toiled along the creek for several winters and then disappeared.

"*Takalu,* the mightiest and eldest of the panthers who reigned over this region proclaimed it was he who chased the workers away," Sani explained. "It was about the time when the sun was at its lowest point in the sky and a full moon shined bright. He stood next to me and raised his voice to the animal kingdom, proclaiming the region free of human infestation. *Takalu* was answered by creatures who were far, far away. So, his voice must have carried a great distance."

"What role could one panther play in chasing the work crews from this site?" I asked, skeptically. "Surely the men carried weapons to protect themselves from the large animals that called this region home. The panther must have been very cunning in order to avoid becoming hunted and killed by the workers."

"I know there were guns, and lots of them," Sani confirmed. "Bradley always carried one, and he rested it against my trunk every time he stepped under my branches.

"*Takalu* claimed he had ambushed one of the workers who walked alone on a dark path. He did it on the night the Timucua called *Soyaluna* to prove to all of the animal kingdom he was more powerful than the humans. The mighty beast decreed it was time for all creatures to return and reclaim their homelands.

[31]"*Soyaluna* was a very mystical and holy time for the Timucua because it marked the end of the dark days of winter and the rebirth of life under a warming sun. It has significance to all living things in nature, too, because the path the sun travels impacts us dramatically. The Timucua spent days celebrating when another winter passed."

"It is hard for me to believe the actions of one panther would drive away the work crews," I interjected. "I'm sure they left because their work was completed, not out of fear of the one animal. "

"You may believe what you wish, Willie. I am just telling you what happened. Twice a year, I feel the *Soyaluna* in my roots and every one of my leaves. It is a time of significance. The workers left and the animals returned to sing *Takalu's* praise for many years."

Sani said the wildlife came back but much of their natural habitat had been destroyed. The land was not the same and never would be. It had been altered forever, as was the habit of all the developers who seemed to come to Florida. The French and Spanish destroyed the countryside to build their initial settlements. The English leveled acre after acre of trees and fauna to make their King's Road so more planters could ravage the countryside to plant cotton, indigo and sugar.

"The peace and serenity of my surroundings disappeared," she said. "Once the canal was finished, there was lots of passenger and freight traffic up and down the canal. The creek I flourished alongside for centuries soon could accommodate crafts much larger than the rafts, canoes and flatboats of the early years. The wildlife stayed as long as they could forage for food and sustain their families. Eventually, as the human imprint became larger, most of them found homes elsewhere.

"When the [32]steamboats began fouling the air with their dark billows of combustion, the face of this land changed again. Population soared, and my beloved surroundings were gone. I realized that was to be the nature of my existence. I learned change is inevitable. I can do nothing but stand here as it happens all around me."

"Yes, humans evolve, as you have witnessed firsthand," I said. "Man continues to invent new things and our technology reaches farther than ever before. I know you are not going to believe this, but I'm going to tell you anyway. John F. Kennedy, our new president has promised that man's horizons will stretch to the moon. He says before this decade is over, an American will set foot on the moon."

"No!"

"Yes! He told the whole world of his plan."

"I thought Superman was an imaginary character," Sani questioned.

"He is," I replied. "Kennedy says we will travel to the moon in spaceships and eventually plant the American flag on the surface. My father believes it will happen. Of course, he is a big fan of JFK because he served in WWII alongside my father. He calls him a visionary."

"I believe anything is possible, Willie. Many visionaries have stepped beneath my limbs. Henry Flagler was a lot like your Kennedy.

"People have been singing his praises for many years. He came ashore here once when he was looking to build his railroad to the uncivilized lands south of here. He remarked on my beauty as his engineers discussed where they wanted to lay his track."

Sani was correct in calling Flagler a visionary, but his vision was much different from that of JFK. Voters put him in the White House in 1960. He never got to see his dreams materialize because he was assassinated in 1962. But we did make it to the moon.

I had learned about Flagler in my Florida History class and he doesn't get enough credit for what he did for the expansion of Florida. Why that man not only had a "[33]Midas Touch" but he must have had a crystal ball, too. He saw opportunity in the wetlands and hammocks of Florida while everyone else saw gators and mosquitoes. When he decided to build a railway from Jacksonville to Miami nobody believed it could be done.

But Flagler was a genius and filthy rich. Before relocating to Florida due to the failing health of his wife, Mary, Flagler partnered with John D. Rockefeller to build Standard Oil into one of the wealthiest companies in the world. Flagler brought an unbridled entrepreneurial spirit to Florida. He joined the group in charge of dredging the East Coast Canal to gain access to the massive land grants being awarded by the state for every mile of waterway that was successfully completed. Using those grants, he forged his fledgling railroad company.

Everywhere the oil mogul stretched his railway, Flagler built a depot and a hotel. And before long the richest families in America were riding his railway and vacationing at his Florida resorts. They came first to St. Augustine and followed Flagler's dash down the east coast of Florida.

The Hotel Ormond was the skyline signature of Ormond Beach for more than 100 years. It was purchased by Flagler two years after it opened and transformed into one of the finest hotels in the world, a playground for the rich and famous of the time. Flagler added three new wings, expanding the number of rooms from 75 to 400, added elevators and a saltwater swimming pool. He built a railroad bridge from the mainland to the doors of the hotel. At the time, it was the largest wooden structure in the United States and included 11 miles of corridors and breezeways. The hotel was located on 80 acres stretching from the Halifax River to the Atlantic Ocean.

Flagler did everything with flare. When he built the Hotel Royal Poinciana on the shores of Lake Worth in Palm Beach in 1894, it had five hundred rooms with indoor plumbing and was recognized as the largest resort in the world.

There was no Miami when Flagler's people began surveying the land for his railway in the mid-1890s. Less than two thousand people resided at the tip of the peninsula. The frontier encampment at the mouth of the Miami River and Biscayne Bay was known as Ft. Dallas until Flagler's East Coast Railway arrived and ignited explosive growth. Today, the region is home to six million Floridians.

[34]Henry Flagler's final and crowning achievement was a project known as "Flagler's Folly," a vision of extending his railway all the way to Key West, at the time Florida's most populace city. Experts said it couldn't be done. Nobody could lay tracks over one hundred and fifty-six miles of ocean, they said. Flagler did it.

In 1912, the Over-Sea Railroad to Key West was completed days after Flagler's eighty-second birthday. It was the most ambitious engineering feat ever undertaken by a private U.S. citizen.

Unfortunately, it never achieved the financial profits Flagler envisioned and was destroyed by a hurricane in 1935. Remnants of Flagler's railway still can be seen today as cars drive between Miami and country's southern-most port.

"I didn't know exactly what that Flagler fellow had accomplished but everyone around here raved about him," Sani said. "He was just one in a long line of builders who passed by here. I figured he must have done something substantial when passersby started referring to this area as Flagler County instead of Mosquito County."

"He was an amazing man," I replied, looking up into the sky and realizing the sun had already moved to the western horizon. That meant it was time for me to head home.

CHAPTER 9

Summer was coming to an end, and I had to spend more time with my chores at our small family farm. It was harvest time and it seemed there always was something to do or pick. In those days, mothers canned a lot of what they grew. Mine was no different. Our garden supplied us with food for the winter months. My mother made pickles from cucumbers and canned tomatoes, onions, peppers, beans and peas. She made the tastiest jellies and jams, too. Her orange marmalade was the best I've ever had. Just thinking about her warm buttered biscuits and marmalade makes my mouth water.

Pop kept me pretty busy for more than a week or so. So, I didn't make it back to the canal for some time. But he dropped me off at the library a couple times when he went into town for supplies. I started studying about Flagler Beach, and how it became a popular gathering place from the very beginning.

Frankly it was an amazing story. I know this because when I related some of the things I had learned to my parents, they agreed. They even thanked me. I felt pretty proud of myself and couldn't wait to get back to the canal and share the information with Sani. Of course, I assumed she was aware of much of the growth because some of it happened not far from where she stood.

First, you must understand not many people lived in this area at the turn of the twentieth century. For decades it had been considered a mosquito-infested swampland with small pockets of population scattered about. Life was difficult because there were no major roads. Supplies had to be carted long distances. Most people who came to Florida arrived by train, and then made their way inland on horse-drawn wagons. For a lucky few, rail cars — pulled by mules or horses over narrow gauge track — were available.

Bunnell boasted the largest population, more than five hundred residents. Other hot spots were Haw Creek, Espanola, Bimini, Dupont, St. Joseph Park and Korona. Of course, lumber and turpentine businesses flourished in the emerging countryside. Citrus was the major crop, but watermelon, potatoes, peppers and cabbage were marketable commodities, too. Farmers discovered Florida's fertile soil would support just about any crop as long as fresh water was available.

[35]It wasn't until 1917 the land between St. Johns and Volusia Counties was given its own identification, a tribute to Henry Flagler. By 1920, the year of the first Flagler County census, there was less than 2,500 people living in the whole county. About 700 lived in Bunnell, the county seat and a hub of activity.

It didn't take long for people to recognize the beauty of the East Coast Canal and the strip of land created between it and the Atlantic Ocean. Just as many Floridians consider Flagler the founder of Miami Beach, Flagler Beach was the brainchild of Bunnell's George Moody. He envisioned it as a tourist location and homesteaded 169 acres along the oceanfront in 1913.

Americans were becoming more mobile, thanks to the Model T Ford vehicles being produced in Detroit. Once the canal was completed, the big problem was crossing it. So, Moody built a ferry large enough to transport one automobile across the canal and a makeshift road across the narrowest part of the marshland. Quickly, the area became popular for residents of the surrounding area, much as it is today. When it took off, Moody reacted quickly. He added a garage, picnic tables, showers and dressing rooms to accommodate the influx of visitors.

Moody's vision became reality in a very short time. People came in droves to [36]Ocean City. Yes, in the beginning it was not known as Flagler Beach. In 1916, Moody built a recreation center he dubbed Ocean City Beach Casino. He outfitted it with a dance floor, a half-court basketball floor, showers, dressing rooms and a refreshment center. By 1920 a fishing pier was added about a block south of where the current pier exists today and construction began on the Flagler Beach Hotel. That was the same year a draw bridge was constructed over the canal. It was a hand-cranked bridge that made access to Moody's recreation area much easier. It was replaced by a drawbridge in 1951.

Flagler Beach was incorporated on April 16, 1925, and George Moody was named the new town's first mayor.

Sani confirmed what I had learned at the library. She said Moody and representatives from the Bunnell Development Company spent lots of time on both sides of the East Coast Canal.

"They had a hard time deciding exactly where they wanted to begin their enterprise," Sani revealed. "They had maps and surveys to study right here under my limbs. I became a big fan of Moody when he told everybody that I might be the most beautiful Live Oak in all of Flagler County, and I was to be preserved at all costs.

"As it turned out, they built south of here and this whole area exploded. Houses began popping up everywhere. I hear human voices everyday now; in the past, I was a special occasion if a human passed under these branches once every full moon."

"Well, I'm glad I happened along at the right time and you decided my voice was one you could embrace," I said with sincerity.

"Willie Brown, you just kept coming back; I couldn't get rid of you if I wanted. Then you stuck than knife in me and forced me to show you the error of your ways."

"Sani, I detect a bit of sarcasm and humor in your response. That's a first. I like it."

"Really? Maybe Huck and Tom have had an effect on me."

"That's a good one, too. Your personality is changing, Sani."

"I don't think so, Willie. I'm just glad you came back. You were gone for more than a few days. I thought maybe you were undergoing another punishment of some sort."

"Well, this is a busy time of the year, Sani," I explained. "It was pretty easy for me to get here during summer, but school will be starting in a couple of weeks. My chores, school and homework are going to take up a lot of my time. I'll probably only be able to get here on the weekends."

"I understand. Your studies are important, Willie. I'll be here whenever you can find time to visit. You must understand, humans lack patience because your time is so short. Surrounded by all of this beauty, time is a wonderful thing for my species. I embrace it, because I know there always are new wonders for me to discover. Waiting is no problem."

"I've never thought of it that way before, Sani," I replied. "Of course, you are right. Everything evolves, and you have experienced great wonders. Thanks for sharing some of your memories with me."

"We have learned much from each other. You have helped me understand the progress humans have made in science and industry.

You helped me understand the world beyond this canal is a fascinating place. I envy you because the expansion of your knowledge is just beginning."

"When I return, I'm going to bring along another of Mark Twain's novels I think you will like. It is "The Adventures of Tom Sawyer." It is every bit as good as Huck Finn, maybe better."

"Oh, that sounds delightful, Willie. I can't wait," Sani said with real joy in her voice.

I bid my friend goodbye and headed home.

* * *

WHEN I ARRIVED HOME, I got the shock of my young life. My father's old pick-up was parked in the front yard with a small trailer hitched to the back. When I ran into the house, I discovered my parents were in the process of packing up all of our household belongings.

"What's going on?" I asked, with what had to be the most startled look on my face.

"We're moving!" my mother declared, wiping tears from her eyes. "Your father has lost his job and we don't have the money to pay the rent. We are leaving tonight. So, you had better gather up the things you want to bring along. I've put some crates and a suitcase in your room."

"But I don't want to move," I mumbled, still in shock.

"What you want at this moment doesn't really matter a whole lot, sonny boy," my father said in a tone that warned me to be wary. "Do your mom and I look happy to you?"

"No, but…"

"No buts! Just do as your mother asked or I will do it for you and you won't like the results. Where have you been all day, anyway? We could have used your help."

"I was down at the waterway…"

"I might have known," my father said, with irritation still in his voice. "I've never known a young'un to spend so much time fishing as you do, Willie. And how many times do you bring supper home for me and your mama?"

"I don't always catch fish," I replied sheepishly.

"That's an understatement!" my father said, seeming more irritated.

65

"Jeremiah Brown stop badgering the boy," my mother said, as she pushed a couple crates in his direction. "He's done nothing wrong. These crates are ready to be loaded on the trailer. Securing the load is your responsibility. Do that and calm yourself. I won't let this move tear this family apart."

My father might have survived a world war and helped repel the Japanese, but he was no match for my mama when she got her temper flared. And I saw fire in her eyes. So, did her husband. He grabbed the crates and continued with the loading outside.

Tears were rolling down my cheeks when my mother wrapped me in her arms to console me.

"There's no shame in crying when you have to leave a place you love, Willie. Your daddy and me have been shedding tears all day while you were off enjoying yourself at your canal. What on earth draws you to that place anyway? Sometimes I think you'd rather be there than in your own bedroom."

"This is one of those times, mama," I said, brushing tears from my cheeks. "That canal is as much a home to me as this house is. I'm going to miss them both."

Just then my father returned and calmly said, "I hear tell there are canals in Ohio, son. There's lots of lakes, too. I'm sure you'll find another fishing spot."

"Is that where we are moving to?" I asked quietly.

"Yes, your father's brother said the steel mills and the automobile industry are booming in Trumbull County, and there are lots of jobs available right now," my mother explained. "You know how good your father is with his hands. He can build anything out of absolutely nothing. Your Uncle Charles said General Motors is building a new manufacturing facility in a place called [37]Lordstown. If that happens, you father could get in on the ground level."

"But that's a long way from Florida," I said.

"It sure is, son, and I'm not looking forward to it any more than you are," my father said, he eyes sorrowful for the first time. "I don't have a choice, though. I have to be able to provide for my family, and this little plot of land – no matter how much we all love it – will not sustain us.

"We need to go as soon as possible so I can line up a job. We don't eat if I don't work. I'm sorry I got a little angry with you before, but I need your support on this. We all must pull together because this isn't going to be an easy move."

"I understand," I said, hanging my head and not understanding a thing. I couldn't imagine leaving without saying goodbye to Sani. Packing up my things was the hardest thing I had ever done. But I headed to my bedroom to begin.

Tears were running down my face when the pickup steered down the dirt road that led away from our tiny farm in Flagler County. As the house grew smaller and dust obscured my view, I tried to transport my thoughts across the marshes to my best friend.

"Goodbye, old pal. Stand strong. When I return, we will talk again."

CHAPTER 10

Ohio was far different than the Florida I had grown to love. But like every other part of this beautiful country we passed on our long ride from Flagler to Trumbull County, there was an abundance of beautiful, green trees. My father got a job right off and we moved into a place called Cortland, where trees were plentiful and there was a huge reservoir nearby. I think the choice of Cortland was intentional, a way for my parents to help me feel at home in my strange, new surroundings.

By the time we got situated, I had a week until school started. I was going into the eighth grade and remember being nervous about fitting in. I think schools back then were friendlier than they are today, and Trumbull County was seeing an influx of new families moving in because of the job expansion of the 1960s.

I liked it right off. Everybody was friendly and I thought the teachers were absolutely fabulous. They all dressed real nice. The women wore skirts and blouses and the men dressed in jackets and ties. It was a lot different than the Flagler Beach School I attended.

There was only about twenty-five students in my whole seventh grade class in Florida. In Ohio, there was three times that many and I worried about knowing everyone's name. They sure knew me, though, because I was the "new kid." I made friends easily and even found a couple buddies to show me where the best fishing holes were on that Mosquito Reservoir.

Do you believe that? I left a county in Florida that once was known as Mosquito County, only to find a sizeable man-made lake by the same name within a mile of my new home. And Cortland was home to more oak trees than I ever imagined. There were no Live Oaks, but there were at least a dozen different species, and I sought them all out.

The White Oak was my favorite. It was the tallest and broadest I found anywhere in Trumbull County. Its branches never reached the size of Sani's but they were sturdy and supported my weight even when I was in high school.

Yeah, I climbed every oak I spotted throughout the Cortland countryside. I always carried a book or comic with me, too. I'd climb up to the strongest branch, lean my back against a firm trunk and read aloud. No matter what I read or how long the words flowed from my lips, no tree ever communicated with me again.

I even carried that old pocket knife with me and stabbed it into a couple of oak limbs with the hope I might get a surly response. It never happened. Sani was one of a kind. I missed her horribly when I first arrived. But as time passed, my thoughts of her became fewer and fewer.

As a teen, I grew tall and agile. All that running to and from the canal turned me into the best quarter-miler in the state of Ohio n 1968. I went on to run for Kent State University, where I met my wife, Linda. We married and had two wonderful children, for whom I have never been prouder.

Until now, I had only told three people about Sani, my high school track coach, Linda and my mother. Coach Jenson laughed and my wife gave me a skeptical stare. Only my mother believed me. She was old and I was a grown man when we were reminiscing about our lives in Florida. One day, she asked me who Sani was.

"Did you have a girlfriend, named Sani, who you used to meet down by that canal you loved so much," she asked.

I was shocked when she spoke her name. So, I asked her why she would ask me such a question.

"I'm your mother, Willie," she explained. "I heard you calling her name in your sleep on more than one occasion. So did your father, but he told me to let it be."

When I told her the truth about Sani, the biggest smile spread across her face, and she said, "That is the most fantastic story I have ever heard. But as far as I know, you never have lied to me, Willie Brown. So, why would you choose to now?"

"I swear, every word is the truth, mother," I said.

"I know it is," she said. "I can see it in your eyes. That twinkle came back when you spoke of your friend. It is the same sparkle I saw each time you returned from that canal. Have you ever thought about going back to see if she still stands?"

"It's been more than fifty years, mother," I replied.

"If what you have told me is true, fifty years is nothing to a species as old as that Live Oak you once loved," my mother said. "You know, your father always said: 'Patience and time can be friend or foe. So, choose wisely.' I think it's time for you to choose.

"Don't you want to know what has happened to her? Don't you want to know if she waits for your return? After all the wonders she revealed to you, how can you not go back to Florida and say thank you? That tree played a part in shaping you into the fine man you are today. Go back, William. It's the right thing to do."

Mama only called me William when she was mad at me or wanted to make an important observation. She made me realize I had unfinished business alongside that canal. And I had no other choice but to return to my beloved East Coast Canal.

I promised her I would plan a trip soon. Her health was failing and I got the feeling she wanted me to do it as much for her as for myself. After all, I had revealed my deepest and darkest secret, and my story did not have a happy ending due to our sudden relocation. I resolved, she was right. It was time to act.

I HADN'T BEEN back to Florida since the day my father's pickup turned north out of our driveway. I flew into Atlanta, rented a car and headed for the interstate highway system that led south. When I got to Jacksonville, I located [38]Scenic A1A, rolled down all of my windows and followed the winding, coastal thoroughfare toward my boyhood home. I wanted to absorb the sights and smells of my drive along the Atlantic shoreline. And they were amazing. I had spent the majority of my life in the Midwest, where steel mills and factories for years had poisoned the air with carbon dioxide, methane, nitrous oxide and other pollutants. When I crossed the state line into Florida I was assaulted with the pungent aromas of plant life and salt water. They reminded me of how much I had missed my boyhood haunts and how happy I would be to walk those game trails and swamplands that led to Sani and my beloved canal.

When I reached Flagler County, nothing was as I remembered it. I marveled at the area's growth. I was awed by the spectacle of Flagler Beach, no longer a sleepy, little beach community but a vibrant city.

I couldn't locate the old farmhouse my parents once rented. Long ago, it had been demolished and replaced by the modern structures that have turned Flagler County in a popular destination for young families and retirees. I marveled at the progressive changes in the landscape.

I quickly realized Sani was right. Change is inevitable. I was determined to find if she was still standing.

When I inquired about an easy route to the East Coast Canal, I was directed to [39]Waterfront Park in Palm Coast, the vibrant community that had spread across the countryside that once was the sole realm of Mother Nature. The beautifully-designed park provided a walking trail along the Intracoastal Waterway that was part of so many wonderful memories from my youth.

As I walked the concrete path that meandered several miles along the waterway, I didn't recognize anything. I began to doubt I would ever find Sani. Expensive homes and condominiums had replaced the thickets, sawgrass, palmettoes and hammocks I once took for granted.

Then, I rounded a bend in the walkway and there she was. Sani's branches still reached far and wide. The walkway now stretched under one of the branches I used to sit on so many years ago. At last, I was home. It felt like that old Live Oak tree was saying, "Hello, Willie! Welcome back!" All I could do was smile as my eyes traveled from her base to her crown. She was larger and more majestic than ever. Her sturdy limbs stretched across the walkway. I imagined they provided shade for hundreds of walkers, joggers and bikers every day.

I had to stomp through a bit of underbrush in order to stand next to her. I was afraid I might be arrested by a park official if I climbed up into her branches. Frankly, I didn't know if my old limbs were capable of making the climb anyway.

So, I wrapped my arms around her trunk and rested my cheek against her warm bark. I breathed in her scent and felt the coarse texture of her bark. Suddenly, the warm flow of energy returned and Sani spoke to me.

"I've missed you Willie Brown. You traveled far away, but your spirit remained here. I knew one day you would return. What wonders have you observed since we last talked?"

(If you enjoyed this climb through Florida history, continue through the footnotes and author's notes for more interesting tidbits. Make sure to leave the author a review at Amazon. He will appreciate the feedback more than you will ever know. Just click the link below.)

LEAVE A REVIEW

FOOTNOTES

[1] Joyce Kilmer (born as Alfred Joyce Kilmer; December 6, 1886 – July 30, 1918) was an American writer and poet mainly remembered for a short poem titled "Trees" (1913), which was published in the collection Trees and Other Poems in 1914. (SOURCE: Encyclopedia Britannica)

* * *

[2] German author Peter Wohlleben has published several books about wildlife. "The Hidden Life of Trees: What They Feel, How They Communicate" is available at electronic bookstores in English translation, along with "The Inner Life of Animals: Love, Grief, and Compassion — Surprising Observations of a Hidden World." Among the revelations in his novel about trees, he points out beech trees are bullies and willows are loners. (SOURCE: The Guardian)

* * *

[3] The Florida Intracoastal Waterway had its beginning toward the end of the nineteenth century, a natural outgrowth of an effort to develop the almost-connected chain of creeks, rivers, lakes and sounds along Florida's east coast into one continuous waterway. The earliest surveys were made in 1844, but nearly forty years passed before construction began. From then until becoming U.S. government property in 1929, the history of the waterway was a continuous fight against vegetation, financing and legislation. (SOURCE: Florida Inland Navigation District)

* * *

[4] Herman Melville (Aug. 1, 1819-Sept. 28, 1891) was an American novelist, short-story writer, and poet, best known for his novels of the sea, including his 1851 masterpiece, "Moby Dick." (SOURCE: Encyclopedia Britannica)

* * *

[5] In Charles Dickens' "Great Expectations," Miss Havisham was a wealthy old woman who wore a rotting wedding gown, having been left at the altar many years earlier. The orphan, Pip, discovers Miss Havisham has never thrown her wedding cake away. It rots and stinks in a corner of the house, a reminder of her unhappy fate. Published in

1861, it is acclaimed as one of Dickens' finest works. (SOURCE: Encyclopedia Britannica)

* * *

[6] The Timucuan Indians had a highly developed, complex social system. They were a strong and aristocratic tribe that thrived in this area for hundreds of years until Ponce de Leon, the Spanish adventurer, arrived. These handsome Timucuans are most often described as tall and strong. The women wore clothing made of Spanish moss. The male leaders were heavily tattooed and wore their hair in "top knots," smoothed with bear grease. They wore ornaments of feathers, shell, bone and fish bladders. The Timucuans used shell and bone to make items like dippers, axes, scrapers, and spear points. Baskets and fabrics were made of palmetto leaves, pine needles and bear grease, and their medical practices equaled those in the Old World. (SOURCE: The New Smyrna Museum of History)

* * *

[7] The book of Jonah is in the Old Testament of the Holy Bible. It tells the story of reluctant prophet being swallowed by a whale. It contains four Chapters, and forty-eight verses. Unlike other Old Testament prophetic books, Jonah is not a collection of oracles but primarily a narrative about the man. (SOURCE: Encyclopedia Britannica)

* * *

[8] The native inhabitants of the region around Plymouth Colony were the various tribes of the Wampanoag people, who had lived there for some many generations years before the Pilgrims arrived. (SOURCE: www.history.com)

* * *

[9] Hundreds of thousands of Indians called Florida home when the Europeans first arrived in the early sixteenth century. But it did not take long for the ensuing wars, slave trade and disease to nearly wipe out the aboriginal population. The natives were decimated by exposure to illnesses for which they had no immunity. Even the common cold was deadly to the native tribes. Armed conflicts with the invaders also contributed to their demise. Natives also were taken as slaves as early as 1520. (SOURCE: Florida Department of State)

* * *

[10] The Seminole Wars (1817-58), Andrew Jackson was at the center of three conflicts between the United States and the Seminole Indians of Florida in the period before the American Civil War. His actions resulted in the opening of the Seminole's desirable land for white exploration and settlement.

The First Seminole War (1817–18) began over attempts by the U.S. to recapture runaway black slaves living among Seminole bands. Under General Jackson, troops invaded the area, scattering the villagers, burning their towns, and seizing Spanish-held Pensacola and St. Marks. By 1819 Spain ceded its Florida territory under the terms of the Transcontinental Treaty.

The Second Seminole War (1835–42) followed the refusal of most Seminoles to abandon the reservation and relocate west of the Mississippi River under President Jackson's Indian Removal Act. The Indians refused, and the war cost the government between $40 and $60 million, the most expensive Indian war in American history. Thousands died.

The Third Seminole War (1855–58) was the result of renewed efforts to track down remnants of the Seminoles who remained in Florida. It caused little bloodshed and ended with the United States paying the most resistant band of refugees to go West. (SOURCE: Encyclopedia Britannica)

* * *

[11] The Bulow Plantation Ruins was designated an historic site in 1954 and is part of the Florida Parks System. It is located off of Old Kings Road, south of State Route 100. The Bulow Plantation Ruins stand as a monument to the rise and fall of sugar plantations in East Florida. It sits on 150 acres, and visitors can tour the remnants of the sugar mill, a unique spring house, several wells and the crumbling foundations of the plantation house and slave cabins. A scenic walking trail leads visitors to the sugar mill ruins, listed on the National Register of Historic Sites. (SOURCE: Florida Park System)

* * *

[12] In Mark Twain's classic "The Adventures of Huckleberry Finn," Huck meets a runaway slave on the banks of the Mississippi River, and an epic journey follows. Twain portrays Jim as a deeply caring and loyal friend who becomes a father figure to Huck, opening the

boy's eyes to the human face of slavery. In reality, both were fleeing the constraints of society, Jim from slavery and Huck from his oppressive family. (SOURCE: Encyclopedia Britannica)

* * *

[13] Thanks to the courage and skill of Barry, both American ships completed their mission and on March 20, 1783, the Alliance sailed into New Port, R. I., abandoning the plan to return to Philadelphia because of the strong presence of a British patrol. (SOURCE: Revolutionary War Archives)

* * *

[14] When Spain's King Phillip II learned a group of French Huguenots had established Fort Caroline in Florida, he was enraged. The French were religious outcasts who wanted to establish a Protestant state in the New World. Phillip, a staunch Catholic, dispatched Don Pedro Menendez de Aviles to rid the New World of the religious zealots. On August 28, 1565 he and his 800 soldiers and settlers created the village of St. Augustine.

Immediately, Menendez attacked and seized the French fort, killing every man but sparing the women and children. He showed no mercy to ship-wrecked French survivors who later arrived at the mouth of the St. John's River. He killed all but a handful. From that day on, the inlet became known as "Matanzas," the Spanish word for "slaughter." (SOURCE: The National Park Service)

* * *

[15] Father Francisco Lopez was the chaplain who accompanying the Menendez expedition against the French. He wrote in a memoir: "Finding they were all Lutherans, the captain-general ordered them all put to death; but, as I was a priest, and had vows of mercy, I begged him to grant me the favor of sparing those whom we might find to be Christians. He granted it; and I made investigations and found ten or twelve of the men Roman Catholics, whom we brought back. All the others were executed, because they were Lutherans and enemies of our Holy Catholic faith." (SOURCE: Eyewitness to History)

* * *

[16] Most Black Seminoles lived separately from the Indians in their own villages, although the two groups intermarried to some extent, and some Black Seminoles adopted Indian customs. Both groups wore

similar dress, ate similar foods, and lived in similar houses. They worked the land communally and shared the harvest. The Black Seminoles practiced a religion that was a blend of African and Christian rituals and their language was an English Creole similar to Gullah. They supported each other in battle and times of need. (SOURCE: Encyclopedia Britannica)

* * *

[17] Florida cattle are one of the criollo-type breeds originally brought to North America by the Spanish Conquistadors in the 16th century. The breed is very closely related to the Pineywoods and Texas Longhorn. Known as Florida Scrub, the cows are a small breed that quickly adapted to the Florida landscape and have long been prized for their resistance to parasites and other hardy traits. They normally weigh under 900 pounds and come in many colors. (SOURCE: Beef2Live)

* * *

[18] In the early to mid-1800's white settlers moved their herds down through central Florida (which was primarily grazing land in those days) to the Caloosahatchee River, and then down the 'Cracker Trail' – a cattle path running from Ft. Pierce to Punta Rassa. From there, they were shipped to Cuba, which had lost a lot of cattle in revolutions. These men, known as "Crackers" because of the distinct sound of their twelve- to fourteen-foot braided whips, would spend many weeks on the trail, sleeping at night on blankets and saddles. In 1838, Punta Rassa became the site of Fort Dulaney, established as a supply depot during the Second Seminole War. By 1840, 30,000 head of cattle were shipped out of Punta Rassa each year. (SOURCE: The Island Sand Paper)

* * *

[19] Florida was the third state to secede from the United States April 10, 1861 and join the Confederate States of America. Census data from 1855 shows 138,000 Florida residents, with 68,000 being slaves. While the state didn't have a great lot of men to join the fight, its agricultural resources were very important to the cause. Florida volunteers served the Confederate war effort by joining what would be referred to as the "Cow Cavalry." Eventually, approximately 900 men enlisted in the 1st Battalion Florida Special Cavalry. Their mission

was to drive cattle and other food supplies north and keep the Confederate Army fed. (SOURCE: www.emergingcivilwar.com)

* * *

[20] The King's Road, which is now surfaced and known as Old Kings Road, is thought to one of the nation's oldest highways. By 1774 much of its construction had been completed, and it provided a passageway from the northern colonies into what was known as *La Florida*. The road connected Colerain, GA, to Cow Ford (now Jacksonville), St. Augustine and plantations to the south. The roadway was reported to be sixteen feet across, with ditches and pine logs laid crosswise in the wet portions. Most of it was an excellent, broken-shell surfaced roadway, well suited to a coach and team. Travelers could follow it as far south as New Smyrna, established in 1768 by Dr. Andrew Turnbull., a wealthy and influential plantation owner. (SOURCE: "Old Kings Road, A Trail Through Flagler County History," by William Ryan.)

* * *

[21] "It was a malaria-cursed desert, a barren wilderness swarming with poisonous snakes and repulsive reptiles," according to travel author Iza Hardy. It was the resounding view of Florida in 1887 held by those in the northern, eastern and western United States. The statement is only one of many negatives Hardy presented in his 1887 book, "Oranges and Alligators." It illustrated the verbal abuse other U.S. regions heaped on Florida. In Hardy's defense, he also wrote about the exotic nature and tropical beauty he discovered on his own journeys through the area. (SOURCE: Digital Scholarship Lab, The University of Richmond)

* * *

[22] Spaniards were passionate about gambling. Men, women and children of all classes and ages played both dice games and board games. In the absence of official game pieces or markers, the residents of St. Augustine made their own. (SOURCE: University of Florida)

* * *

[23] The divide between the Matanzas and Halifax Rivers was the most difficult dredging of the entire Intracoastal Waterway. Time being money, the canal company directed their efforts to the south where construction was much easier and a whole lot faster. For investors,

each mile of completed canal was rewarded with a payment of almost 4,000 acres of land. The state paid only when a mile of dredging was completed. (SOURCE: Flagler Beach Museum)

* * *

[24] During the 1600's, Ponce de Leon Inlet – south of Daytona Beach — was most likely a haven for English pirates, who repeatedly attacked the Spanish colony of St. Augustine. Sir Francis Drake, a favorite of Queen Elizabeth I, was one such pirate. New Smyrna was described as "a safe port for the English privateers to slip into; here they could, with all ease, lurk for the rich Spanish ships coming from Havana through the Gulf of Florida." In 1682 Spanish Governor Cabrera in St. Augustine reported the English had killed 10 Indians at Mosquito Inlet and had taken fifteen others as slaves to be used as divers. This was notable because the privateers used Indians to recover treasure from sunken Spanish galleons. (SOURCE: New Smyrna History Museum)

* * *

[25] "The noise produced by the clashing of the shells and the scrambling of many flippers on the loose sand when a shoal of turtles crawls onto a beach during a dark night can be quite terrifying to a novice at "turtling" because he cannot tell what produces it, and it is a sound quite unlike anything he has previously heard." (SOURCE: Turtling in Florida, by J.M. Murphy, Tales of Old Florida, 1987 by Castle Books)

* * *

[26] "Jack and the Beanstalk" is an English fairy tale that first appeared in 1734. It was rewritten several times. Joseph Jacobs rewrote it in English Fairy Tales (1890) and his version is most commonly reprinted today. In the tale, Jack trades a cow for some magic beans which he plants. Overnight the seeds grow and reach the sky. When Jack climbs the bean stalk he finds a castle, a giant and many treasures. (SOURCE: Wikipedia)

* * *

[27] "The Last Days of Superman" was released to the public in October of 1962. It was a collaboration by science fiction writer Edmond Hamilton and artists Curt Swan and George Klein. It is a classic from the Silver Age of Superman comics. Collectors everywhere covet Superman #156. (SOURCE: DC Database)

* * *

[28] In 1881, a group of St. Augustine residents led by Dr. John D. Westcott incorporated the Florida Coast Line Canal and Transportation Company and the Florida legislature authorized the firm to dredge a series of canals to create an inland waterway along the length of the Atlantic coast. As an incentive, the state granted 3,840 acres of land for every mile of canal constructed and gave the company the right to collect tolls on the waterways.

The State had millions of acres of public lands, which they frequently deeded to rail, navigation and other companies to spur development. In 1885, the stated deeded the canal company 87,670 acres of public lands. Dredging operations picked up considerably over the next five years moving south, and in 1890 the state deeded 345,972 acres to the company.

In 1892, Henry Flagler invested in the firm and a year later became president for a brief time in order to expand his railway. The dredged canals and connected waterways became known as the Atlantic Intracoastal Waterway, ultimately linking Jacksonville to Miami in 1912. (SOURCE: University of Florida Library)

* * *

[29] Coquina is a mixture of sediment and shells deposited and compacted along the waterways of Florida for centuries. When quarried or mined, it is relatively soft until allowed to dry. Then, it is suitable for building. Coquina forms the walls of the Castillo de San Marcos in Saint Augustine. Derived from the Spanish word for cockle or shellfish, coquina made excellent material for forts, particularly those built during the period of heavy cannon use. Because of coquina's softness, cannonballs would sink into it, rather than shatter or puncture, the walls of the Castillo de San Marcos. (SOURCE: National Park Service)

* * *

[30] George Lothrop Bradley, third son of the late Chief Justice Charles Smith and Sarah (Manton) Bradley, was born in 1848 and died in 1913. He was president of the Florida Canal Company and the company's largest investor. A friend of Alexander Graham Bell, Bradley started the New England Telephone Company in 1877 and merged with the Bell Telephone Company in 1879, earning great profits. (SOURCE: Wikipedia, Find A Grave Memories.)

* * *

[31] The sun is the source of light and life for all things on the planet, and it has been worshiped by people around the globe for centuries. *Soyaluna was* the astronomical event we know as solstices and equinoxes that mark the path the sun travels. At the summer solstice, the sun is at its highest point in the sky. At the winter solstice, it is at its lowest. The spring and summer equinoxes mark the midway point of the sun's movement between the solstices. (SOURCE: The Spiritual Sun.)

* * *

[32] A New England steamboat company advertised a schedule of hefty charges to transport passengers and freight on the waterway between Titusville on the Indian River and Palm Beach on Lake Worth, with thirty-three stops in between. A passenger traveling the entire distance — spanning some 143 miles — would expect to pay $4.30 for the trip, with an extra charge of seventy-five cents for a meal. A single stateroom berth cost an additional dollar, while the charge for an entire state-room called for another $2.00. Each passenger was permitted 150 pounds of baggage without extra charges. (SOURCE: The Papers of Albert Sawyer)

* * *

[33] The "Midas Touch," or the gift of profiting from whatever one undertakes, is named for Midas, the legendary king of Phrygia. Midas was granted the power to transmute whatever he touched into gold. Phrygia is part of Turkey in today's world. (SOURCE: www.mythweb.com)

* * *

[34] Henry Morrison Flagler was born on January 2, 1830 in Hopewell, New York, to Reverend and Mrs. Isaac Flagler. At the age of 14, after completing the eighth grade, Flagler moved to Bellevue, Ohio where he found work with his cousins in the grain store of L.G. Harkness and Company, at a salary of $5 per month plus room and board. Later he partnered with John D. Rockefeller and became one of the country's richest men before dying at age 83. Flagler fell down a flight of stairs at Whitehall, NY, where he made a winter home. He never recovered from the fall and died of his injuries on May 20, 1913. He was laid to rest in St. Augustine. Flagler County was named in his honor when the county was created from portions of St. Johns and Volusia Counties in

1917. ("Last Train to Paradise," Les Standiford, Crown Publishing 2003; Flagler County Historical Society.)

* * *

[35] Flagler became a county in 1917 as a result of residents wanting to govern themselves. The new county was made up of southern portions of St. John's County and a northern patch of Volusia. The communities of Bunnell, Espanola, St. Johns Park, Haw Creek, Dupont, Korona and Ocean City (Flagler Beach) were the economic and population centers at the time. Bunnell became the county seat. (SOURCE: Flagler Library Friends)

* * *

[36] Austin Vanburen Wickline, who had resided in Dupont and Haw Creek for a short time, built the first home on the Atlantic side of the canal in 1913. It was located on Lambert Street about 300 feet north of the present bridge. Once they relocated, the Wicklines added a room that was used as the beachfront's first store. The Ocean City Post Office was established in 1915 and housed in the Wickline store. Mrs. Wickline, the former Esther "Etta" Chaffee, was appointed Postmaster. (SOURCE: Flagler Beach Museum)

* * *

[37] The Lordstown Complex is a General Motors automobile factory in Lordstown, Ohio. At one time, it included three facilities: Vehicle Assembly, Metal Center, and Paint Shop. The plant opened in 1966, restructured to build the Chevrolet Cruze compact car at the time of this publication. It now closed its doors completely. (SOURCE: General Motors Media)

* * *

[38] Perhaps no stretch of highway reaches further into America's history than the A1A Scenic & Historic Coastal Byway. Scenic A1A stretches for 72 miles from the seaside luxury and golf mecca of Ponte Vedra Beach to Gamble Rogers Memorial Park on Flagler Beach. Mostly two-lane highway, the road connects state parks, national monuments, stunning beaches, nature trails, boating, fishing, preserves and estuaries. (SOURCE: Florida's Scenic Highways)

* * *

[39] Waterfront Park opened in September of 2010. The $1.9 million park spreads over almost 21 acres along the Intracoastal Waterway. It

is bounded on the north by properties owned by the Florida Inland Navigation District and the Forest Park gated development, and to the south and west by the Grand Haven gated development. It is located off Colbert Lane, about a mile south of Palm Coast Parkway. (SOURCE: City of Palm Coast)

NOTES FROM THE AUTHOR

I learned so much about Florida in writing "Tree of Wonders," it turned into a labor of love. I've always been a fan of history and learning about the state I have chosen as my final home was long overdue. I hope it was informative and entertaining for you, too.

Of course, I reminisced about some the classic novels of my youth – "The Adventures of Huckleberry Finn" and "Moby Dick" — in an effort to maintain the exchange of information between Willie Brown and Sani. So, I guess this is as good a place as any to apologize for including "The Last Days of Superman" in that list. It pales in literary prominence to the aforementioned classics, but it was one of the classic moments of my adolescence. To make up for it, here's a bit of trivia you can use on your grandfather, grandmother or anyone born in the1950s or earlier: Who made up Superman's Legion of Super Heroes?

Keep reading. The answer is forthcoming.

* * *

AS ONE MIGHT imagine, Florida is rich in history and legend. Unfortunately, there is little record of the natives who inhabited the land a thousand years ago. Florida's consuming environment, greedy plantation owners and modern land developers destroyed countless Indian burial grounds and antiquities that might have given greater clues to the ancient people who walked the land before the white man arrived.

Nonetheless, there were many interesting facts, events and legends that passed before my eyes as I researched "Tree of Wonders." Many simply did not fit into to the dialogue between Sani and Willie Brown. That's why I added almost forty footnotes and these notations.

* * *

WRITTEN HISTORY OF Florida begins in the sixteenth century, precisely in 1513 when Spanish explorer Juan Ponce de León landed on the peninsula and informally named it La Florida (Land of Flowers). La Florida exemplified two of Spain's colonial objectives: forts to protect the valuable exports from Mexico and Peru; and the development of missions to fulfill the Pope's charge to the Spanish Crown of converting the native peoples to Roman Catholicism.

Early explorers were accompanied by priests and followed by missions and missionaries, sent to the New World by the various religious orders. Many missions failed until the founding of Saint Augustine by Pedro Menéndez de Avilés, who raised crosses at various points in Florida and south along the coast of the Atlantic Ocean.

* * *

AFTER THE SPANISH annihilated the French at Mosquito Bay (now Matanzas Inlet), they did little to move southward into what we now know as Flagler County. The entire region was referred to as the Mosquito Swamp and deemed impossible to navigate. Their only intrusion was to build an outpost at the mouth of the St. John's River to protect Castillo de San Marcos from marauding pirates and the covetous English. It is now known as Fort Matanzas and is part of the National Park System. Visitors must take a free boat ride across the inlet to gain entry to the ancient fort.

* * *

THE ENGLISH RULED Florida from 1763 to 1784, accepting the unsettled but fertile territory in a "land swap" with Spain, whose flag had flown from the peninsula for 198 years. After years of conflict, Spain surrendered Florida in exchange for the rights to the Philippine Islands and Cuba. Of course, Florida remained loyal to King George during the American Revolution. At the conclusion of the conflict, all British subjects were ordered to abandon their lands and slaves when England ceded Florida back to Spain in 1784. Florida remained under Spanish rule until 1821 when the expansionist Americans acquired Florida and the Oregon Territory in the Treaty of 1819.

* * *

THE ACQUISITION OF Florida by the United States prompted the migration of thousands of American planters into Middle Florida, the region bounded on the west by the Apalachicola River and on the east by the Suwannee.

Cotton became the major cash crop and large numbers of African slaves toiled on plantations owned by the planter elite. On the eve of the Civil War in 1860, enslaved persons made up more than half of Middle Florida's population.

* * *

EIGHTEENTH-CENTRY FLORDA provided Europe with three commodities that were in high demand – sugar, indigo and lumber from the Live Oaks that grew in abundance. The tree's dense, hard wood was important for ship-building worldwide. Air-dried, a cubic foot of Live Oak could weigh as much as fifty-five pounds.

In fact, the British built a large lumber mill, called Hewitt's Mill, near where Pellicer Creek crosses U.S. 1 today. The waterway then was known as Woodcutter's Creek, according to Flagler Historian Al Hadeed.

* * *

DR. ANDREW TRUMBLL founded the Florida settlement of New Smyrna in 1768. He brokered a deal with British Gov. James Grant to extend The King's Road south to his new settlement to support his highly profitable plantation. He used indentured workers from the island of Minorca and imported slaves to help in the construction, promising them land of their own in exchange for their labor. Few payments were made. His efforts, though, were integral to the extension of the roadway.

* * *

THE KING'S ROAD created a passageway for migration into the Sunshine State from the northern colonies. Runaway slaves, freed men and women and disenfranchised natives also sought refuge in the untamed wilderness where they could assimilate into the sparsely populated landscape. They were welcomed by the Seminole Indians, a mix of many different tribes that had been chased from their native lands to the north and west by white settlers. By 1831, there were approximately thirty-five Seminole villages in northern Florida with about 5,000 inhabitants.

* * *

WITH THE EMANCIPATION of slave labor following the Civil War, Florida underwent another metamorphosis. King Cotton gave way to the influence of northern capital. Railroad lines and roads expanded deep into the Florida peninsula. Wealthy northern families purchased large tracts once used for cotton cultivation and converted the land into hunting plantations.

Northern Florida became known for quail hunting. Quail inhabited areas covered with longleaf pine trees and wiregrass. In order to bolster quail populations, owners of large estates maintained extensive tracts of indigenous forest through the practice of controlled burning.

* * *

LIFE IN FLORIDA was difficult for the Black Seminoles, and many left Florida for Coahuila, Mexico in 1849. They were led by John Horse, also known as Juan Caballo. In Mexico, the Black Seminoles (known there as Mascogos) worked as border guards protecting their adopted country from attacks by slave raiders. By 1858, fewer than 200 Seminoles remained in Florida.

When slavery finally ended in the United States, Black Seminoles were tempted to leave Mexico. In 1870 the U.S. government offered them money and land to return to the United States and work as scouts for the army. Many did return and serve as scouts, but the government never made good on its promise of land. Small communities of descendants of the Black Seminoles continue to live in Texas, Oklahoma, and Mexico.

* * *

BEFORE THE CIVIL WAR, the United States was easily the largest importer of Cuban goods, especially cigars. When hostilities erupted between the Spanish colonial government and Cuban nationalists in the 1860s, hundreds of thousands of Cubans fled their island homes. They immigrated to Europe, other Latin American cities, New York City and Florida, bringing with them the knowledge of cigar-making.

In 1867 alone, more than 100,000 Cubans fled the embattled island. A large portion of the skilled laborers came to Florida and planted the seeds of the cigar industry, which flourished immediately.

* * *

THE REGION SOUTH of Matanzas Inlet, including most of what is now Flagler County and farther south, was named Mosquito County. The territory that makes up most of Flagler was controlled by massive sugar plantations. Bulow, Mala Compra and St. Joseph were the major settlements. All were wiped out during the Second Seminole War (1835-1842). The conflict was the fiercest war waged by the U.S. government against Native Americans, who were being resettled to the West in accordance to the Indian Removal Act of 1830, driven by expansionist President Andrew Jackson. It was also considered the largest slave uprising in history. The United States spent millions fighting the Seminoles. It became the most expensive war against native people in U.S. history. The war left more than 1,500 soldiers and American civilians dead. At its conclusion, most of what is now Flagler County laid in charred ruin and the region was almost completely depopulated.

* * *

DURING WORLD WAR II, the waters off Flagler Beach and the entire U.S East Coast were a breeding ground for enemy activity. German submarines began patrolling the American coastline in 1942. Their mission was to disrupt shipping lines by sinking defenseless transport ships. For a time, they were successful.

Nazi U-boats sank 274 ships off the east coast in June of 1942 alone, 216 of them were in Florida waters. A report in the May 14, 1942 Flagler Tribune stated the situation briefly: "From information available it appears the Florida coast has become one of the most active fields for Nazi submarines, ships being torpedoed with disturbing regularity."

The U.S. Coast Guard set up surveillance of the region from a station located where Gambill Rogers State Park now sits.

* * *

NO, I HAVEN'T forgotten to leave you the answer to my Superman trivia question. Here it is: Cosmic Boy, Saturn Girl, Lightning Lad, Sun Boy, Brainiac 5, Bouncing Boy, Triplicate Girl, Shrinking Violet and the Invisible Kid made up Superman's Legion of Super Heroes.

FACT OR FICTION

The more I researched Florida, the more I learned. Here is a smattering of unusual facts I found interesting, and I hope you do too:

■ Made mostly of Florida pine, The Belleview Biltmore Resort and Spa, northwest of Tampa Bay was said to be the world's largest occupied wooden structure at 820,000 square feet.

■ The Everglades National Park encompasses 2,100 square miles and contains the largest mangrove forest and the slowest moving river in the world.

■ The St. John's River is the largest in the state and one of only a few that flows north to south.

■ Stephen Foster, who wrote "Old Folks at Home," Florida's state song, never even saw the Suwannee River, nor did he ever step foot in Florida.

■ Florida has 1,197 miles of coastline and 663 miles of beachfront.

■ Florida produces about seventy-five percent of all U.S. oranges and forty percent of the world's supply.

■ The state boasts over 30,000 lakes and more than 1,000 golf courses, most of any state in the nation.

■ A bald cypress was thought to be world's oldest tree. "The Senator" resided at Big Tree Park in Longwood, Florida until it was destroyed by vandals on January 16, 2012. Experts estimated its was 3,500-years-old and stretched 118 feet into the sky. Believe it or not, it was burnt to the ground by a woman lighting a crack pipe inside The Senator's hallow trunk.

■ Florida is similar in size to England and Wales combined.

■ No matter where you are in Florida, you are never more than sixty miles away from the ocean.

THE END

ABOUT THE AUTHOR

Gerald L Guy is a retired newspaper editor who lives in Palm Coast, FL with his wife, Joanne. He was the recipient of numerous state, regional and national writing awards during his long journalism career. His pursuit of words began as a sportswriter in his hometown of Warren, Ohio. Guy eventually edited daily newspapers in Ohio, Georgia and Wisconsin.

He retired in 2004 and moved to Florida the following year. When he's not writing or editing short stories and novels, he's walking the scenic trails and sunny beaches of Flagler County.

"Altered Lives" is his first foray into the mystery genre, although characters in most of his books have been confronted by the evil deeds of mankind.

He is the author of more than a dozen novels that include three trilogies, novellas and stand-alone titles.

In 2019, he published "Act of Mercy" and "Act of Recall" to go along with "Act of Kindness" and complete his Coastal Capers trilogy. All three capture the spirit of a mysteriously active, retirement home resident who thrives on helping others.

The Gus McIntyre Adventure Series includes four titles and a fifth is in the works. "Run to Danger" and "Run Like the Wind" were the first two and re-packaged into "PAYBACK: Eye for an Eye" for marketing purposes. In them, an orphaned teen tries to find his way in the often-lawless West of the 1870s. "Chasing Gold," a semifinalist in the prestigious Laramie Awards for western writing, and "Chasing the Past" complete the series.

The Wolf Pact Saga, a fantasy about a shapeshifting people who live in secrecy in rural Wisconsin, began in 2011 with "The New Order" and was followed by "Escape from Captivity" and "Dream Catchers."

An independent author, Guy published "Tree of Wonders" in 2018. In 2016 he released "SARA: A Hero's Story," historical fiction that traces the actions of the crew of the *U.S.S. Saratoga CV-3*, an aircraft carrier that helped win World War II. The author's late father, Ralph G. Guy, served aboard the Sara and remains his hero today.

Guy published "Secrets of the Heart," his first entry into the romantic genre, in 2020. It is a novella about two senior citizens who find romance in their golden years and try to keep it a secret from their children. It's for sale at Amazon or can be downloaded for free at his web site.

In 2021. the author published "Altered Lives" in January, a cold case mystery about an ex-Army Ranger who discovers on his twenty-fifth birthday his biological family was brutally murdered in Ohio. He heads to his birthplace to uncover a murderer in hiding.

Additionally, Guy expects to publish "New Paths," the next entry in The McIntyre Adventure series.

REVIEWS

Reviews by readers are the fuel that sustains independent authors. The more reviews an author collects, the more prominence and promotion are awarded by most electronic bookstores.

So, reviews are the best way you can tell an author "Thank you!"

A review can be as simple as: "I liked it!" or a critical assessment of any length. You can leave them at the site where you purchase a book, at Goodreads, Facebook, Twitter or at my website.

Believe it or not, I relish your negative comments as much as those that are positive. It helps me connect better with my audience. Just click the link below:

LEAVE A REVIEW

PREVIEW

The first two books in The McIntyre Adventures, are available in this boxed set. They include "Run Like the Wind" and "Run to Danger." It has attracted audiences from young teens to senior citizens. It is on sale at Amazon for Kindle and Kindle Unlimited readers,

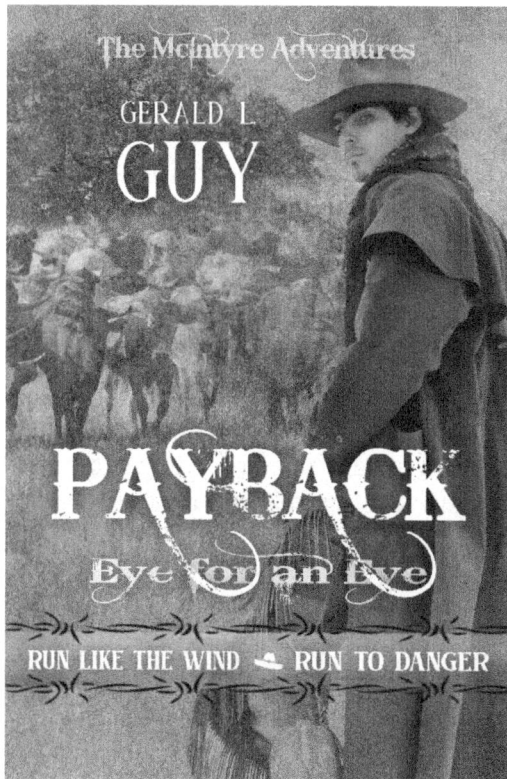

Run Like the Wind

CHAPTER ONE

The call of cattle lowing carried across the dark hills in the still morning air like a rooster claiming its turf on any farm in nineteenth century America. The morning was anything but routine for Eongus "Gus" McIntyre, who was suddenly awakened by friendly sound. He had been searching for civilization for more than a week. Had it found him? Could it be true or was he imagining things?

He listened carefully and was positive it was the low rumbling of cattle being rousted from sleep as the sun began to make its bright presence known across the eastern horizon. Not so long ago, fourteen-year-old McIntyre took dawn's awakening for granted on the farmlands of the Illinois River. That's where his family plied the rich soil for more than a decade. Now, it was music to his ears, especially if it meant cattlemen were pushing livestock to nearby pastures.

He rolled up his blanket, gathered his meager belongings and started to run toward the familiar sound. His pace was swift and quiet. His grandfather always said his grandson could "run like the wind." He prayed he could run even faster today so he could catch up with the herd and hopefully be rescued by whoever was prodding livestock toward winter feeding grounds.

He was eager, but apprehensive. The Black Hills had been anything but friendly to him so far. Ten days ago, almost exactly six weeks after he and his father had left their Illinois farm to seek their fortune in the lucrative gold mines of the Black Hills, they had been attacked by bandits. His father was killed, and Gus was abandoned along the trail. He was lucky to have survived the ambush and had been wandering for days, keeping a close eye out for Indians and outlaws.

When his father steered their horse-driven wagon into the Black Hills, it was the rampaging tribes he most feared. As they reached the Nebraska Territory, they had been told of a major upheaval in in the Montana Territory, west of the Dakotas. General George Armstrong Custer and his entire cavalry unit had been wiped out in the summer of 1876 at a place called the Little Big Horn.

"Don't worry, Gus. We'll be hundreds of miles east of Montana when we arrive in Deadwood," his father said, his eyes sparkling when he spoke of their destination. "Keep your eye out for Indians just the same. They've been known to kill any white man they find trespassing on their land, and they think all of this is their land."

Waving his arms with excitement, James Sr. added, "They can have all of it except the small piece you and I stake as our claim. We're gonna be rich, son. No savages are gonna stop us."

Just two years earlier, it was Custer who confirmed the presence of gold in the Black Hills, aggravating the Sioux Nation with the rush of humanity to their sacred land. It was September now, three months since Custer met his demise. The Black Hills oozed with unrest.

Unfortunately, it was white men the McIntyres should have feared most.

When the attack began, his father ordered Gus to run, and he did. He couldn't remember running any faster or being more scared at any time in his short life. He hid in the forest for a full day while the outlaws ransacked their wagon and tortured his father.

"Give us your gold or die," the leader of the gang ordered.

"I ain't got no gold but I'm fixin' to get me some if you boys let me go," the elder McIntyre pleaded. "I just left my Illinois farm two months ago. I'm on my way to find my fortune."

"Then today is not your lucky day," the outlaw with long red hair and a shaggy beard bellowed just before shooting Eongus James McIntyre Sr. in the forehead. They left him lying there in the dirt while they laughed and rummaged through the belongings they had packed for what his father called "the adventure of a lifetime."

Gus went unnoticed in a thicket not far from where his father lay dead. He didn't emerge from his hiding spot until he was positive the outlaws had departed for good. Then, he crawled out and tended to his remains. He pulled a blanket over his lifeless body because he couldn't stomach looking at his only kin in such a bludgeoned condition. The bullet had torn off half of his father's face.

Gus buried his father with a shovel he found among the family's scattered belongings. The outlaws had not only taken his father's life, but they took everything of value brought from Illinois. Guns, ammunition, food and supplies were all gone.

Young Gus spent another day at the burial site, mourning the loss of his only relative and trying to figure out what to do next. He constructed a small cross and planted it at the gravesite before striking off in search of his destiny. He had no desire to mine for gold, but he knew he had to locate civilization in order to survive.

* * *

THE BLACK HILLS, most of which rises from the plains of Nebraska and are located in what is now known as South Dakota, presented the young teen with a challenge. They stretched over more than one hundred square miles of wilderness in 1876. It certainly was no place for a fourteen-year-old farm boy. Long considered the sacred land of the Lakota Sioux Nation, the lawless territory was infested with gold thirsty settlers, angry Sioux renegades and outlaws of all kinds.

Young Gus McIntyre was raised comfortably on the rich farmlands of Illinois. He could read and write and was taught at an early age to sustain himself in the fields or the forests. While his father provided his knowledge of farming, young McIntyre inherited a love of the forest from his grandfather, a third-generation American whose ancestors emigrated to the New World from Scotland in the eighteenth century. They helped settle the frontier lands west of the Appalachian Mountains. Thanks to his grandfather, Gus could track and hunt, find and build shelter and live off the land if needed.

He was an expert marksman but had no gun or ammunition. His tool of defense was a slingshot his grandfather taught him to use long before he was strong enough to raise a firearm in his tiny hands. It gave him a bit of confidence as he wandered through the forest-covered hills and valleys. He knew he could find game, and he was deadly accurate with the rock-thrower. A hunting knife was his only real weapon, and it always hung at his side.

Autumn had almost completed its transformation of the Black Hills. The leaves had turned color and the nights were growing cooler. In another month there could be snow on the ground, a fact that made Gus' search for civilization more urgent.

Each night when he fell asleep, the young teen dreamed of home, a tiny farm along the Illinois River where he and his parents had enjoyed a wholesome life. Influenza had taken the life of his mother and grandfather in 1874 and devastated his father. Eventually, it was "gold fever" that hastened the death of Jamie McIntyre. Gus never felt so alone.

Thankfully, he was no stranger to the wilderness. He knew where to find edible roots and that he could chew the bark of most pines and birch trees for nourishment. But he relied on his trusty slingshot, a constant companion in his hip pocket, to provide protein. Like most regions of the western frontier, small game – rabbit and squirrel — were plentiful.

For water, he stayed close to the creeks and streams that flowed generously through the Black Hills. The nights were growing cold and the water was clear and refreshing.

It was the Y-shaped weapon that saved his life when he was about a week into his journey. Because the nights were growing cold, Gus had secured a blanket of moss he wrapped in his blanket to keep him warm each night. It also helped him blend into the environment.

The largest animal Gus had seen during his wanderings was the whitetail and mule deer of the region. The streams he followed teamed with fish and were natural gathering places for animals, large and small.

Gus was sound asleep one night beneath his mossy comforter when he heard something rummaging through his stash of nuts and berries. He opened his eyes to discover a large bear gorging itself on his breakfast.

As quietly as possible, he discarded his blanket, sat up and loaded the slingshot. When he yelled "SHOO BEAR!" the beast turned on him and growled menacingly. That's exactly when Gus released the sinew that propelled a round piece of granite at his nemesis. It struck the bear square in the snout. The young grizzly howled in pain, dropped the basket of berries and ran off across the stream and into a thicket.

Gus gathered what was left of his breakfast and climbed a nearby tree. He stood watch the rest of the night, but the bear never returned. That's when he decided to follow the path of the stream but make his nightly camp far from its shoreline.

Every other day or so, he made his night camp on one of the hills so he could look over the terrain that lie ahead. He was high on one of those dark mounts when the sound of the cattle gave the enterprising boy hope. As he skirted along an animal trail that led north, he thought the sounds were getting closer. The low rumbling sounded like the call of a mother to her young calf. His heart raced. He increased his pace and fixed his eyes on the horizon.

When he found the herd, it was in a valley a mile away. He waved his arms and called to the cattlemen who were driving the cows north. Of course, they could not hear him above the din of the lowing and pounding of hooves. He had to get closer.

It took him about no time to make his way down the rocky slope to the valley floor. He found some of the drovers gathered at a covered wagon for lunch. His excitement was overwhelming. Finally, he had found other humans.

He had spent ten days wandering and the entire morning chasing the sound of livestock. Now, it was time to make his presence known and seek the help of others.

CHAPTER TWO

Gus could hardly contain his joy as he approached the covered wagon where a couple of riders laughed with a gargantuan black man. He had a full beard and odd-shaped hat, made from the fur of some sort of animal. Gus had never seen the likes of it. It seemed poised and ready to attack from atop the giant Negro's head. One of the riders, a burly man with dark hair, sipped coffee from atop his horse, while a thinner and younger man dipped a ladle into a pot simmering over a campfire. Whatever was cooking smelled delicious. Gus' mouth watered.

As quietly as he could, he snuck closer to the wagon. When he was within twenty-five yards of the three strangers, he stepped out of the brush to announce his presence. Before he could utter a word, a lariat circled his body and yanked him off his feet.

"Hey look what I caught sneaking up on you boys," declared a tall blond-haired cowboy, seated atop a tan horse. Gus hadn't seen him approaching. The cowpuncher who had been sipping coffee immediately yanked a pistol from his holster and aimed it at the teenager.

"Hold on! Hold on!" the black man called out. "He's just a kid!"

"I don't care who or what he is," the coffee-drinker said. "Anyone who sneaks up on me is likely to get shot. These hills are teaming with outlaws and redskins. How do we know he's friendly?"

The black man stepped between Gus and the gun-toting wrangler. "The boss ain't gonna like it if'n you shoot an unarmed kid, Buck. Why don't you give me a chance to find out what he wants?"

"Toots, you know better than to step in front of my pistol," Buck replied. "You're lucky I didn't shoot you."

"Hell fire, Buck! You ain't gonna shoot nobody, especially me. You love my cookin' too much. Now put that gun away."

The black man stood well above six feet. Gus guessed his stride was twice the length of his own as he lumbered toward him, his shadow blocking out the sun. "Let off that rope a bit, Clint. I'm gonna help the boy up and see what he's doing out here in the middle of nowhere," he ordered.

Gus' joy quickly turned to fear. He was shaking when the black man reached down, pulled the rope over his head and tossed it back to its owner. He grabbed him by the shirt collar, helped him to his feet and said, "Okay, mister! Who might you be? And why are you sneakin' up on my chuckwagon?"

"Ah... Ah... I'm Eongus James McIntyre... Please, don't shoot... Need help... Men killed my daddy... I've been lost for days and..."

"Slow down, kid," Toots said. "Come over here and have something to eat and tell me and the boys what misfortune has befallen you. We're not gonna do anything to harm you," the black man said with a smile that helped chase away McIntyre's fear.

The cook's big, right hand wrapped around Gus' upper arm to ensure he didn't run away, and he used his left to clean off the seat of the boy's pants. Toots dragged him to the campfire, threw a biscuit and a pile of beans on a plate and said, "Sit right there on that log and put some grub in your belly. I'll grab you a cup of coffee and you can tell us what's goin' on and why you showed up here in the middle of the Black Hills. Mind you, though. I want you to do your eatin' and explainin' slow like. You're among friends, son."

Gus swore the ground shook each time the big man took a step, but the plate of food garnered his full attention. The beans were too good to ignore. They were cooked in molasses and mixed with venison. It was absolutely the finest-tasting food Gus had consumed in an awfully long time. As he took the last bite of the biscuit he said, "This is good! Thank you."

Seated in the middle of the three cowboys and the cook, Gus told his story. They found it hard to believe one so young could survive in the wilderness for ten days without a weapon or knowledge of the terrain.

"What did you do for food?" one of the cowhands asked.

"I scrounged some wild root vegetables my grandfather taught me to search out," he replied, "and I got me a squirrel almost every day. I cooked it over a small fire, hoping nobody would spot me.

My father warned me there were lots of Indians roaming these hills."

"How is it you were able to shoot a squirrel? You ain't got no gun," a cowboy named Billy asked.

Gus proudly pulled the slingshot from his back pocket and held it up for everyone to see.

"It's perfect for small game and it makes no sound," the greenhorn informed. "Lucky for me, there's lots of squirrels in these hills and valleys. I only shot what I could eat."

"I'll be tarred and feathered," Billy said. "Let me see that thing."

Gus passed it to the friendly wrangler who must have been in his early twenties. He watched him spin it in his hands and draw back the sinew as if he were taking a shot.

"I used to have one of these when I was a boy. We used to shoot cans with 'em. Never was good enough to shoot a squirrel. You must be one heck of a shot, kid."

"My grandpa made it for me, and he was a good teacher," the boys said and blushed a little. "I don't' miss too often."

Billy handed him back the peashooter and said, "Let's see how good you are. You got a pebble in your pocket?"

"Always!" Gus replied.

Billy threw what was left of his coffee on the ground and stood up. Gus knew what was coming and he loaded a small stone into the pouch and watched the man rise to his feet. He quickly glanced at Toots, who smiled and nodded.

"I'm going to toss this here cup in the air. You shoot it. I want to see if you're as good a shot as you say," the cowboy said.

"Why would I lie about something like that?" Gus asked.

"I didn't say you was lyin', boy. Just want to see how good ya is. Are you ready?"

"I'm always ready," Gus said with confidence. He squeezed the perfectly carved handle with his left hand and held the stone and pouch in his right. When the cowboy hurled his coffee cup, he shot just before it reached its peak.

When the stone hit the tin cup, it made a sharp ringing sound and found a new flight path. It landed behind the chuckwagon in a fresh pile of horse dung.

While the other cowboys marveled at the shot and laughed at the consequences, Billy fumed.

"Dad-gummit, look what you did, kid!" he said.

"Sorry! You should have thrown it out into the open."

"Boy's right, Billy. I'd suggest you go retrieve your cup and clean it good before it melts right into those droppings. If that pile was left by old Bessie, it's dangerous stuff," Toots said with a big smile.

Everybody laughed at Billy's expense as he sauntered over to rescue his cup, mumbling expletives under his breath.

"And that's exactly why I drew iron on the boy," Buck said good-heartedly. "I'm lucky he didn't come into this camp firing that thing. He'd a put my eye out."

"That was my fault," Gus admitted and hung his head a bit. "I should have known better than to barge in on you all. I was just so glad to find people. I wasn't thinking straight. And I wouldn't have shot at any of you."

"He's just joshing you, Gus," Toots said. "We're glad we were here at the right time for you to find us. Buck wasn't going to shoot you. He ain't never shot nobody."

"I know, but you gotta understand," Buck said, "When it comes to Injuns and outlaws, he who hesitates generally ends up dead, just like your daddy. The Black Hills is no place for greenhorns. You're lucky to be alive."

"Shucks, Buck. I think the boy knows that already," Toots said. "You don't have to be so darned straight forward. He's just a kid who has suffered greatly."

"Sorry, boy. It's the only way I know," the tough said.

"It's okay," Gus replied. "I'm sorry I surprised you. I was really excited and just wanted to hear a friendly voice.'"

"Did you recognize any of the men who assaulted you and your father?" Toots asked.

"No, sir! But I would know the one in charge, the man who shot my father, if I ever saw him again," the fourteen-year-old replied. "He had red hair like mine, a big beard and a scar that stretched from his right temple to his chin. He was mean looking, and I'll never forget his face."

"Don't you fret. He'll pay for what he done," the cook said. "The Good Book says, 'vengeance shall be mine.'"

"It also says something about an 'eye for an eye.'" Gus chimed in. "My grandpa told me that. I think that's fair."

"Whatever you are thinkin', boy, wipe it from your thoughts. A vengeful man has a hard time findin' peace," Toots said.

The youngest of the three men, the man who was eating when Gus walked in on the group, introduced himself. He stuck out his hand and said, "They call me Junior because my father oversees this cattle drive. Let me assure you, there is nobody on this drive who will hurt you, and we'll give you all the help you need."

"I'm Gus. It's easier than Eongus, and that is what my momma and daddy always called me. My dad only called me Junior when he was mad at me. Does your father do that with you?"

"No, the old man calls him worst names than that when he gets upset," Buck said with a laugh.

"Speakin' of the old man, here he comes now." Toots said. "He's probably wonderin' what's takin' you guys so long to get back to work."

"You best get along before he gets here. I'll tell him we've got a visitor," Junior said.

All three mounted their horses and rode out toward the herd. Junior stopped to chat with his father before following the other hands to the cattle that were moving slowly through the valley.

"You don't have anythin' to worry about, son," Toots said. "This is a pretty good bunch of fellas. If it is help you need, you've run into the perfect outfit. The Circle H Ranch turns its back on nobody in need.

"Mind my word, though. The old man is a hard one. Grip his hand firmly when you introduce yourself and be respectful. That is Walter B. Hamilton III. I call him Mr. H. You best call him Mr. Hamilton."

Hamilton rode in atop a big, white stallion. It was the most beautiful horse Gus had ever seen. The boss wore silver spurs and a silver belt buckle that reflected the sharp rays of the autumn sun. He sheathed a Winchester rifle before dismounting.

The trail boss looked at Toots and then at the boy. "Is the coffee hot, Toots?"

"You know it always is, Mr. H," the cook replied.

"Then give me some and tell me who this greenhorn is," Hamilton said as he swatted dust from his Stetson and ran a kerchief across his brow.

"My name is Eongus James McIntyre, Mr. Hamilton, and I'm in need of a little bit of help," Gus said, reaching his hand out to the imposing foreman.

"Well, that's what I understand," Hamilton said, impressed by the kid's firm grip. "Do you know anything about cattle, son?"

"No, sir, but I'm willing to learn."

"Well, we'll see about that," he said as he drained his coffee cup. "Mighty good coffee, Toots. Thanks! You're in charge of this young'un. Teach him all you know and keep him out of trouble until we get to Deadwood."

"That's what we'll do, sir," Toots replied.

"See you in a few hours when we bed this bunch down for the night," Hamilton said as he remounted and rode out of camp. "Glad to have you aboard, Irish!"

When only the cook and Gus were standing at the campfire, he asked, "Does that mean you and me is partners, Toots?"

"I think it does."

"He was mistaken when he called me, Irish?" Gus asked. "My family hails from Scotland, and my grandad always told me to make sure people know the difference. He didn't have much love for the Irish for some reason."

"That's good to know," the cook replied. "People make all kinds of assumptions when they first look at ya. That red hair atop your head signals you ain't from here.

"Names mean a lot. Make sure you set the boss straight the next time you see him. He won't take offense, and it'll make everyone else abide by your wishes."

"What does your name mean, Toots?"

"It means mind your own business," the cook said as he lifted the pot from the hot coals. "Douse that fire and I'll start packing this rig so we can move up the trail and get ready to feed this bunch supper."

Gus smiled. It felt good to have a full belly, new friends and chores to attend as trainee for the Circle H Ranch.

READ MORE

THE GERALD L. GUY COLLECTION

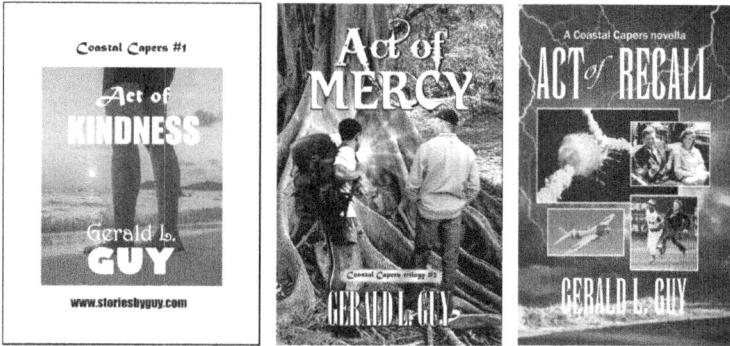

COASTAL CAPERS

Act of Kindness — Nobody at Crater Lake Retirement Center could believe Jerome Browning was 92 years old. He looked and acted much younger. Still, he devoted his life to helping residents restart their lives. Fighting a dysfunctional director every step of the way, Jerome and a wealthy benefactor find innovative ways to bring joy to shattered lives. Browning had no idea how an ancient curse and a simple act of kindness would turn his own world upside down.

Act of Mercy – A simple act of kindness led Jerome Browning to prosperity he never imagined possible. When a root he finds washed up on the Atlantic shoreline grows into a modern day "beanstalk," his world is turned upside down. Accompanied by a blind, one-armed teenager, Browning is required to travel through strange new lands, negotiate with otherworldly creatures and avoid disrupting history to outsmart a corporate behemoth and save the world's oceans. It might be beyond one man's capability.

Act of Recall — Who is John Doe VI? Can a pair of binoculars, his friendship with Jerome Browning and months of therapy unlock the past for the newcomer at Crater Lake Retirement Center? When his memory returns, he discovers a gruesome past and a family he had long forgotten. Will it bring horror or joy?

THE WOLF PACT SAGA

Wolf Pact: The New Order — When W. Jefferson Prescott III is introduced to a species of wolf that can alter its genetic makeup in order to walk as humans, he discovers a magical world and a second chance at life. His predestined rise to power creates chaos and unity. While Jefferson must learn the ways of the four-legged Cossibye, his three companions — Aponi, Shideezhi and Skilah — struggle to embrace life in Jefferson's human world. This cultural collision, combined with the discovery of amazing physical and sensual powers, takes readers on a journey of fantasy, romance and mystery.

Wolf Pact: Escape from Captivity — After rescuing abused siblings on a dark Wisconsin night, the Cossibye clan is catapulted into a search for the orphans' relatives and face off with a madman who is leaving dead bodies and shattered lives wherever he travels. With the help of the children's father — Michael Mangus Walker — Jefferson, Sebby, Sherry and Reeny must rely on cunning and all their special powers to preserve the children's safety and return peace to the plush Wisconsin countryside.

Wolf Pact: Dream Catchers — A 600-year-old shaman of the Osage Nation is wreaking havoc in Wisconsin. As the body count grows, the press thinks a werewolf might be stalking students at

Marquette University. The Cossibye have no other choice but to join the investigation and end the senseless murders before one of their own is harmed or killed? New friends, Carl Birdsong and Cheyenne Konti, help the blend ancient potions with modern technology to preserve peace.

THE MCINTYRE ADVENTURES

Run like the Wind — Fourteen-year-old Eongus "Gus" McIntyre suddenly is orphaned and abandoned in the Black Hills, the wildest and most untamed territory in 1876 America. Luckily, he is befriended by a group of cattlemen who are driving 100 head of Texas Longhorns north to feed hungry gold miners in lawless Deadwood. An ornery trail cook, named Toots, and the boss' son, Junior Hamilton, take young McIntyre under their wing. With the help of irascible Calamity Jane, the youngster earns respect, avenges his father's murder and starts a new life.

Run to Danger — Rustlers and Mexican vaqueros threaten the livelihood of the Circle H Ranch in 1877, making young Gus McIntyre's job of rounding up stray Longhorns more than challenging. An aging Apache chief comes to Gus' rescue, and together they plot revenge and secure the Hamilton assets. In the process, long-standing animosities between their white and native cultures begin the healing process.

Chasing Gold – When a dying stranger slips a mysterious map into the hands of young Gus McIntyre, it sets he and his friends on an incredible journey to find the hidden wealth of Mexican Emperor Ferdinand Maximilian. Government agents and ruthless vigilantes from the Ku Klux Klan want the gold, too. When his life and the lives of those he cares most for are threatened, where will Gus run to avoid danger? Will his race to find the treasure end in hardship or happiness?

Chasing the Past – Gus McIntyre's great-great-great grandfather, James Oliver McIntyre, fled Scotland to find adventure and romance in the New World. He also found hardship and friendship while blazing trails west with none other than Daniel Boone. Gus tells his story as he searches for a new beginning in nineteenth century Texas.

PAYBACK: Eye for an Eye – A boxed set of the first two Gus McIntyre Adventures that was released in October of 2019 for Kindle and Kindle Unlimited readers.

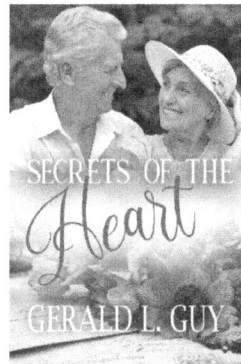

OTHER TITLES

SARA: A Hero's Story — When the Japanese attacked Pearl Harbor in 1941, the men of the U.S.S. Saratoga CV-3 fought back. This work of historical fiction chronicles the role "The Mighty Lady" and her crew played in bringing about an end to Japanese terrorism and World War II. The historical tale is based on the memoirs of dozens of veterans who served valiantly aboard the venerable aircraft carrier. One of those brave men was the author's late father, Ralph G. Guy. Most of his shipmates have passed away or are in their twilight years. All remain heroes from a time too often forgotten.

Tree of Wonders — Have you ever looked at one of Florida's ancient and majestic Live Oak trees and wondered what they might reveal if they could talk? Young Willie Brown finds the Tree of Wonders on the banks of the Intracoastal Waterway, and it reveals tales of yesteryear..

Learn about the native tribes that inhabited Flagler County, how sugar turned sour for early plantation owners and how transportation played an important role in the region's depopulation and rebirth.

Secrets of the Heart — When Annie Coldwater's daughters discover their late mother had a secret love affair, they are shocked. They assumed she was too old and too gray for such shenanigans. But when a stranger shows up at the funeral home and spends a long moment at their mother's casket, questions arise.

Author Brian Warren met Annie at a book-signing, and they fell in love immediately. He denies her nothing, including the secretive nature of their romance. That all changes when Annie suddenly dies, and Brian decides some secrets are best revealed. Then, all hell breaks loose.

Altered Lives — On his twenty-fifth birthday, Georgian Matthew Brownlee is informed by his adoptive mother that he had been misled about the sudden death of his biological parents. They were murdered on Halloween 1981. After being informed of a massive inheritance, Matt requests and is granted his discharge from the U.S. Army and heads to Ohio with sister Betsy to search of the killer or killers of a family he never knew.

In 2006, newcomers to the tiny community of Kinkaid OH make tongues wag. When activity stirs around the home at 69 Oak Hill Drive — the site of the grisly murders — the sleeping community awakens.

Can Matt use his Army Ranger training to breathe new life into the cold case? What secrets are neighbors hiding? How many more lives will be altered in his quest for justice?

Autographed copies of all the author's novels can be purchased at his website. Got to:

www.storiesbyguy.com

Made in the USA
Columbia, SC
26 February 2022